TOO HOT TO SLEEP
Stephanie Bond

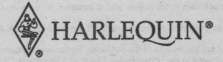

D0101255

⬧ HARLEQUIN®

TORONTO • NEW YORK • LONDON
AMSTERDAM • PARIS • SYDNEY • HAMBURG
STOCKHOLM • ATHENS • TOKYO • MILAN • MADRID
PRAGUE • WARSAW • BUDAPEST • AUCKLAND

This book is dedicated to Chris,
my telecommunications story consultant
and permanent love-scene research partner.

ISBN 0-373-25887-9

TOO HOT TO SLEEP

Copyright © 2000 by Stephanie Bond Hauck.

Visit us at www.eHarlequin.com

Printed in U.S.A.

1

GEORGIA ADAMS GNAWED on her thumbnail as she read aloud the instructions for her new deluxe telephone answering system in hopes the words would make more sense the third time through. "When you select the dial pad mode, you are toggling the live dial pad option. When live dial pad is on, the hands-free option is activated if the auto answer feature was previously selected. See page 38-B, diagram H." Georgia pursed her mouth, then mumbled a curse word that was not in the manual, although she planned to call the company and suggest they include a handy reference page for expletives as soon as she got the bleeping phone working.

After hitting the "clear programming" button, she unplugged all three cords and started over at the beginning of the dog-eared book. Ninety minutes and six fingernails later, she achieved a dial tone and shrieked with success. Doing a victory dance on her sisal area rug, she spiked the instruction manual and gloated when it landed near her VCR that, after three years, still flashed "12:00." Thank goodness her VCR and television had been spared during the electrical storm that had zapped her phone. Positive that any minute she'd mysteriously lose the ability to dial out, she dropped onto her hard couch and dialed her friend Toni's number.

"House of bondage," Toni answered.

"You are terrible," Georgia said, laughing. "What if this had been Dr. Halbert calling you in to work?"

"I'm not going even if he does call. I wouldn't miss this bachelorette party for anything."

Georgia cleared her throat. "About the party—"

"Oh, no you don't, Georgia Arletta Adams! You're not backing out on me."

"How did you find out my middle name?"

"The question is, how many people in the hospital ER will I tell if you don't go with me tonight to Bad Boys? Besides, Stacey will be crushed if you don't show."

"Stacey will be smashed and won't care."

"Oh, come on, Georgia, have some fun. Afraid Rob the Blob won't want you ogling naked, sweaty, muscle-bound men?"

Georgia shifted on the firm cushion in a vain attempt to find a comfortable position, then reached to straighten a picture on her side table, one of her photographic creations. "No. Rob's working late and said he didn't mind if I went."

"Good grief, woman, you mean you really asked him?"

Actually, she'd secretly hoped he'd be the slightest bit jealous, especially since she'd yet to see *him* naked after ten months of dating. Instead, he'd sounded surprised, but added that he wasn't the jealous type. He *trusted* her, for heaven's sake—how patronizing. "Asking him was the considerate thing to do."

"It was the pathetic thing to do. The man doesn't own your orgasms."

You're telling me.

"Besides, what the heck else are you going to do tonight?"

Sleep sounded good, but Georgia recognized the early signs of insomnia by now and knew she'd be wide-eyed most of the night. She floundered for a chore that sounded remotely engrossing. "Program numbers into my new phone."

Toni scoffed. "Which will take all of ten minutes."

"Not for the gadgetronically challenged like myself."

"Pshaw. I'll expect you at my place in one hour. Show some skin and bring plenty of one-dollar bills."

Georgia mumbled goodbye, then frowned at the handset, searching for a disconnect button. These newfangled portable models would make slamming down the phone obsolete. Not that she was the slamming sort, but at thirty, she expected many character-building experiences ahead of her and it seemed prudent to keep relevant props nearby. Fumbling for a button would not have the same impact.

At last she hit the Talk button, surprised when she heard the resulting dial tone. Her confidence bolstered, she pushed the programming button and after a few minutes of jockeying with arrow keys, managed to enter the numbers of the people or places she dialed most often: Rob, Toni, her mother, her sister, the personnel office at the hospital, various friends, the pizza delivery place, the Thai delivery place, the Chinese delivery place and the Mexican delivery place. Then she jotted down the names and corresponding two-digit numbers on the little pullout tablet on the base station, the most impressive doohickey on the entire gizmo, in her opinion.

Georgia wiped the perspiration from her forehead with the hem of her T-shirt. Was it her imagination, or was her apartment the hottest spot north of the Equator? From her vantage point, she could see the blasted programmable thermostat in the hall. The building manager had reset it for her three times and the place still felt like a sauna. Oh, well, she'd look for *that* instruction manual tomorrow—she might be on a technological roll, but she didn't want to push her luck tonight. Besides, sweating was good for the pores.

She leaned her head back on a stiff cushion, thinking how much she'd grown to loathe the beige sectional sofa. Two years ago she accepted her registered nurse's position in emergency medicine. When she had first moved to Birmingham, Alabama, leaving behind her mother and sister, she'd bought ultramodern living room furniture for her apartment as a symbol of her newfound independence. Soon, however, she'd come to realize that the harsh lines and drab colors were less than friendly when settling in to watch a classic romantic movie. On the other hand, Rob said he found her furniture a welcome change from the flowery styles preferred by most women.

Georgia smirked, thinking that Rob's preference for furniture could also describe his preference for sex—the man was a minimalist. A heartbeat later, she regretted the thought because Rob Trainer was a hardworking, ambitious accounting consultant and a consummate Southern gentleman. Well, maybe *consummate* was an unfortunate word choice.

An overhead stretch to pull her tired shoulders turned into a full-body yawn. Her insomnia, combined with Rob's gentlemanly ways, was testing her physical endurance, which was precisely why she'd prefer to skip the party at the male strip club. She pulled a hand down over her face, trying to squash the provocative images swirling in her mind, and the quickening in her thighs. She'd never been to a strip club, but she had a bad, bad feeling that such a place would only fuel the flame in her belly she was trying desperately to smother.

She pushed herself to her feet and strolled the perimeter of her living room, opening windows to let in air an nth degree less stagnant than the air inside her tiny third-floor apartment. Thick and pungent, the evening wafted indoors. Street noises rose up to lure her outside—revving engines and bright lights and blaring horns and booming stereos, scantily dressed women laughing and calling to men driving convertibles and straddling motorcycles. Everyone was in search of sex on this hot, southern night.

Including Georgia Arletta Adams.

She sighed and pressed her nose against the window screen. Even people close to her would be shocked if they knew that she, Nurse Goody-Two-Shoes and everybody's little sister, suffered from her own private affliction: a breathing, burning, pulsing, vigorous, distracting, overblown sex drive.

She stopped short of calling herself a nymphomaniac because she wasn't promiscuous. In fact, she had a reputation for being a bit of a prude, which, she'd discovered years ago, was an effective safeguard against a dangerous tendency. She had simply refused to bend to the will of her restless body.

Oh, there'd been a couple of unremarkable encounters with other grad students in college, and one or two brief relationships since. But the men hadn't excited her, hadn't tapped into her secret garden.

Georgia walked to the kitchen and opened the refrigerator door, sighing with relief when the cool air hit her skin. She lifted the tail of her T-shirt to cool her stomach, then removed a banana from the crisper to munch while her refrigerator worked overtime.

She eyed the banana and sighed—everything looked phallic these days. She bit off the end and fanned her shirt. By immersing herself in work, she'd managed for the most part to keep a lid on her powerful urges...until a year ago. Then, triggered by either the surge of hormones most women experience in their early thirties, or years of repression, or this damnable relentless southern heat, her body had launched a quiet rebellion.

Georgia had always assumed she would marry one day, but she'd stepped up her efforts to find Mr. Right, thinking that exploring her fermenting sexuality would at least be safer within the confines of a monogamous relationship. Rob Trainer had seemed like the perfect candidate: handsome and successful, well-mannered and reflective, intelligent and friendly. She liked him immensely. But after investing the past several months in their relationship, she had come to one conclusion: the man had no interest in sleeping with her.

She was ripe for the picking, and he seemed content to walk around the tree.

And, if truth be known, it was more than the sex she craved—it was the closeness, the intimacy generated when two loving people shared sex. The tingly "you complete me" stuff she saw in movies but observed between too few couples these days. If the specter of true love still existed, she wanted it. Matchless love, not the desolate, co-dependent relationship her parents had passed off as a marriage. She wanted a man who would lower his guard, a man who would make a fool out of himself for her, a man who would cherish her.

Georgia sighed and fanned herself. Meanwhile, that inner rebellion was now reaching cataclysmic proportions. During her nursing studies, she'd read documented cases of spontaneous combustion. At the rate her internal furnace was stoking, and with no end in sight to the scorching summer heat wave, she feared she might be approaching flashpoint.

She finished the banana, and reluctantly closed the refrigerator door, then studied the deep crimson pedicure on which she'd splurged in the feeble hope that Rob nursed a foot fetish. But last night he hadn't even blinked when she'd worn her new strappy high heels. Instead he'd warned her about falling and breaking her neck, then suggested that she double-check her disability insurance coverage and kissed her on the cheek. She'd never thought of herself as the kind of woman who would end a relationship because the guy wouldn't take advantage of her, but she had needs that were clamoring to be met. Somehow she had to find a way to let Rob know she was ready to take the next step, and soon.

She made a face at her sofa as she passed through the living room on her way to the bedroom. Soon, too, she'd buy a comfortable couch, but for now, school loans and tips for nude dancing men took precedence. Georgia idly lifted her long hair from her moist neck, winding it into a loose knot. She dreaded the evening, and fervently hoped she wasn't about to ignite a blaze Rob might not be able to put out.

2

"COME ON, GEORGIA, stop gawking and start squawking!" Toni laughed and dragged Georgia to her feet, then cupped her hands over her mouth and hooted at the gyrating man on stage. The naked bodybuilder wore a headdress and twirled a short stick with fire at both ends, seemingly oblivious of the danger to his lineage. He moved across the stage in little hops to the beat of the calypso music blaring from speakers at deafening decibels. His body was remarkably muscled and proportioned to the point of deformity. Georgia could only stare, and Toni cheered like a woman who'd never before seen a baton.

In fact, the entire room undulated with hundreds of standing women, their hands raised to offer tips, their voices lifted to offer encouragement to the men who performed on the U-shaped runway. Of course, the dancers didn't require much urging to remove every stitch of clothing and wag the audience into a frenzy. The throbbing music and high-pitched screams reached such a staggering crescendo, Georgia was certain the shaking mirrors that flanked the stage would shatter at any moment.

She suddenly swayed and grabbed the back of the chair in front of her for support. Embarrassment rolled over her in waves. Every square inch of her skin tingled. Her breasts felt heavy and, since the room was stifling hot, she couldn't blame their hardened points on the cold. Her stomach swam with dizzying desire.

Georgia held her breath and allowed the atmosphere to consume her. The scent of the performers' body oils, the taste of perspiration on her upper lip, the press of bodies around her, the flashing spotlights that criss-crossed the room, the pulsing music, all swirled around her like a haze of sexually charged ions. It wasn't so much the dancers' naked bodies but the blatant openness that she found so titillating, the fact that the men were proud of their physiques, and that the women weren't afraid to express their appreciation.

Georgia wet her salty lips. It was enough to drive a decent woman to do things she might not ordinarily do.

She fumbled behind her for her untouched rum drink. Curving her hand around the cool glass, she lifted it to her feverish cheek. Georgia glanced at Toni to see if her friend had noticed she was quietly freaking out, but Toni was laughing and waving dollar bills.

Thinking the alcohol might numb her too-keen senses, Georgia gulped the drink. The fire twirler exited in a blaze of glory, only to be replaced by a construction worker with a swaying tool belt. Within minutes, he had stripped down to his hard hat and was taking bids from the women on the perimeter of the stage. Georgia felt a tingling in her thighs and frustration crowded her chest. She tried to project Rob's face onto the body of the dancer, but she couldn't reconcile the two separate images of stability and sensuality.

"Some hammer, huh?" Toni asked, nudging Georgia out of her reverie.

"Hmm?" Georgia scanned the man's considerable attributes. "Oh, yeah, I guess." She drained her glass in another deep swallow.

"Hey, are you okay? I was just teasing about Rob earlier. Did you guys have a fight or something?"

"No."

Toni's eyes narrowed and she jerked her head toward the ladies' room.

Georgia grabbed her purse and followed a bit unsteadily, sensing an inquisition but grateful for the break from the onslaught of erotic cues.

Before the door closed behind them, her friend had lit a menthol cigarette. Georgia frowned, then opened her purse and retrieved a lipstick. "I didn't know you smoked."

Toni exhaled and leaned her rail-thin body against a condom vending machine. "Special occasions only. So, are you having a good time?"

She ran a finger around the collar of the sleeveless white button-up shirt she'd worn tucked into loose black jeans. "Sure."

"Liar. You've been in another world all night."

Her heart pumped the rum through her body, bypassing her empty stomach and sending the alcohol straight to her brain, making her feel floaty and somewhat philosophical. "I have the all-overs."

Toni squinted. "The all-overs? Funny, I don't remember that one from school."

Georgia turned and stared at her flushed reflection in the mirror and talked while she drew an uneven line of mocha lipstick onto her mouth. "I'm restless, fidgety, distracted."

"Horny?"

Leave it to Toni to cut to the chase. She sighed, puffing out her cheeks, liking the way her laugh lines disappeared. "Toni, do you think I would know if Rob was gay?"

Her friend choked, then coughed out a cloud of smoke. "Probably. Why would you think that?"

She blotted the lipstick with a rough paper towel. "I don't really. It's just that I can't figure out his...likes and dislikes."

Toni chortled and dismissed Georgia's concern with a wave. "They all have hang-ups, babe. My old boyfriend liked Aerosmith on the stereo when we made love. Go figure." She pressed fingers to her temples and closed her eyes. "Let me guess. Rob wants the lights off, and his socks *on*."

Georgia gave her a wry smile. "I wouldn't know."

Her friend's eyes bulged. "You mean the two of you have never had sex?"

"Right."

Toni pursed her lips. "Wow. How far have you gone? Second base? Third?"

Georgia quirked her mouth side to side. "I've never been quite sure what constitutes second and third base."

"You're stalling."

"Okay, we've kissed."

"No uncontrolled groping?"

"No."

"No nipplage?"

"Nada."

"No oral sex?"

She shook her head.

"Damn, no wonder you think he's gay. But I have a lot of homosexual friends, and I'd bet money that Rob is not gay."

Georgia tilted her head and inspected her own reflection. "Which means he doesn't find me sexually attractive."

Toni's face appeared over her shoulder. "Look at you—great hair, great face and great body. I'm telling you, the man is probably intimidated."

She rolled her eyes. "Oh, yeah, that's me, Miss Intimidation. I'm not exactly a siren, Toni."

"Precisely. Most of the time you look like Miss Untouchable." The cigarette bobbed wildly. With a flick of her wrist, she removed the clip that held Georgia's dark hair away from her face, then fluffed the long layers. "And here." Toni removed a cranberry-colored lipstick from her purse. "Toss that brown stuff and try this."

Georgia applied the new color, then frowned. "It's bright."

"Yes, ma'am." She twisted Georgia sideways, then unbuttoned her white shirt until the little pink bow on her bra was exposed. "Do you have to wear the bra?"

"Yes!" Bare skin under thin white cotton? Oi.

"Okay, okay." Toni pulled out Georgia's shirttail

and tied the front ends high enough to expose her navel. "There. You just need to loosen up. I'm sure all Rob needs is a signal."

She looked back to her reflection and pursed her mouth. "You think?"

Toni dotted the cranberry lipstick onto Georgia's cheeks, then blended the color with her thumb. Someday her friend would make a wonderfully smothering mother. "Definitely. Do something to shake him up a little. You know, show up at his place wearing nothing but a belt or something like that."

Georgia chewed on her lip. "And what if he turns me down?"

Toni shrugged. "It'll be his loss and then you'll know where you stand. But trust me, he *won't* turn you down."

Her friend had a knack for making things seem so black-and-white. And even as her tongue formed more words of protest, Georgia stared at her new wanton image in the mirror and warmed to the possibilities. She'd worked her way through college and three years of post-graduate work. Every day she handled life-threatening situations at the hospital. So why would she be worried about making a pass at a man she'd been dating for several months? Maybe because it was safer to let him go on thinking she was Miss Modesty than to risk unleashing the passion that boiled beneath the surface. She didn't want to come across as some kind of...well, any of those names her mother had called her father's string of faceless girlfriends.

"Come on," Toni said, snuffing out her cigarette.

"Let's buy Stacey a table dance—I saw her eyeing the pirate. Besides," she added with a wink, "we have some planning to do."

Georgia followed her friend, rubbing the headache forming just behind her ear. While most people had a conscience, her *conscience* had a conscience—a something that reined in her urges, and kept her on her best behavior.

She swallowed. At least so far.

GEORGIA SLIPPED INSIDE her apartment door and swatted at the light switch. Still buzzing slightly from her last drink, she kicked off her shoes next to the couch and glanced at her new phone contraption, but the message light wasn't blinking. How flattering. She removed the portable phone from the base and headed for the bedroom, not the slightest bit sleepy. In fact, her pulse kicked higher with every step.

Over the past few hours, she'd thought about Toni's advice and allowed herself to be carried along on the crest of the erogenous wave rolling through the strip club. She'd decided her friend was right—Rob was waiting for her to make a move. So, during a shared cab ride home, Toni had settled upon the least threatening, yet highly erotic option: phone sex.

Despite that phone sex was a favored fantasy of hers, Georgia felt obligated to protest on behalf of the upstanding girl she was purported to be. Besides, she didn't know how to do it.

Toni had pshawed. "What's to know? You talk, you moan, you hang up."

"But how do I ask him if he wants to?"

"Don't ask, just *do*."

And if Rob were totally offended, Georgia reasoned, she could always move to the Midwest and change her name.

Moving slowly in the dark, she slipped out of her shoes. Could she pull it off? The fact that she'd never participated in phone sex before only heightened her anticipation. Her chest rose and fell more rapidly, her breasts tingled, her thighs grew moist.

She turned on a lamp, then dimmed the illumination to bathe her Verdigris iron bed and the mustard-colored comforter. After stepping out of her jeans and folding them over the padded seat of her vanity table, Georgia sat on the edge of the bed and sank her crimson-tipped toes into a green hooked rug she'd made when she was fifteen—a lifetime ago. At that age she had fantasized of romance and physical bliss, never imagining one element without the other. She had thought by now she would've met a man who could provide a constant supply of both. Could Rob?

She sighed. Well, soon enough she would know if her fantasies would get him off, or scare him off.

Georgia glanced at the clock. One-thirty, Wednesday morning. Rob would be in deep REM sleep. Although if things went to plan, he'd be wide awake within a few seconds. Before she had time to reconsider, she slipped off her white cotton panties and left them lying on the rug. Her hands shook slightly as she held the phone and pushed the button to retrieve Rob's preprogrammed number.

When his phone began to ring, warmth flooded her abdomen. After the third ring, she panicked and started to hang up, but before she could locate the darned Talk button, she heard his sleep-fuzzy voice come over the line.

"Hello?"

Her heart thudded so loudly she could barely hear him. "Hi, Rob, this is Georgia."

"Hmm?"

"D-don't talk," she said, then leaned back against a pile of pillows and lowered her voice to what she hoped was a sexy tone. "Just listen."

3

AFTER SIX YEARS on the police force, Officer Ken Medlock should have been used to late-night calls, but he still had trouble focusing on the voice at the other end of the line. He reached for the lamp on the nightstand, but remembered a split second after the sound of the hollow click that he'd forgotten to replace the burned-out bulb.

Did the woman say she was "Georgia"? His mind spun as he tried to place the name—a new dispatcher? Blinking seemed to help clear the cobwebs. One-thirty. Damn, the last time he'd looked at the clock had been less than an hour ago. His intermittent insomnia seemed to have grown worse as the temperature climbed—and now this interruption.

"Rob, I know it's late, but I've been thinking about...us...all evening and I was wondering...that is..." The woman with the sultry voice inhaled and Ken opened his mouth to tell her she had the wrong number.

"I'm not wearing panties."

His mouth snapped shut and his manhood stirred, proving at least one part of his body was processing information.

A small trembling laugh sounded. "I've always wondered if you were a boxer man or a brief man."

What was the mystery woman's intention? Engage in a little late-night dirty talk to entice this Rob guy to come over? "Boxer," Ken blurted, then swallowed and leaned back onto his requisite three-pillow stack. Had he lost his mind? Or more appropriately, had he lost his shame?

"Mmm. Do you sleep in them?"

When I sleep. He couldn't remember such a welcome interruption though—few of his *dreams* were this good. He might have thought his partner was playing another practical joke on him, but even Klone wouldn't go this far. And the woman sounded so sincere, she had to be the real thing. His job required him to make life-and-death split-second judgments, but suddenly he was gripped with indecision—'fess up, hang up, or play up.

His body made the decision by sending a flood of desire to swell his deprived loins. What would be the harm in succumbing to one wild impulse? Before he had time to reconsider, he muttered, "Mmm-hmm." Knowing she might realize her mistake any second, he held the mouthpiece a few inches away from his mouth. On the other hand, if she didn't know what kind of underwear Robbie Boy wore, maybe she'd just met the man. Or maybe she was a prostitute. Ken had lived in the South for most of his adult life, but had never met a woman named Georgia.

"I thought it was time to let you know how I feel."

Or maybe her boyfriend simply didn't know how good he had it. "Okay," he offered.

"But not if this makes you uncomfortable."

He found the crack in her confidence endearing.

Did she have any idea how sexy her voice sounded? And the only thing uncomfortable at the moment was his hardening erection. "I'm fine. Um...go on." When silence followed, he was afraid she was onto him.

"Can you shed those boxers?" she whispered.

In for a penny, in for a pound. Ken reached beneath the warmish pilled sheet and slid off his shorts in three seconds flat, not an easy feat in a waterbed while juggling a phone. The TV remote he'd left on the bed crashed to the wood floor. "They're gone. Are—" Ken wet his lips, "are you undressed?"

"Not yet," she said. "I'm wearing a white button-up blouse and a white bra."

Ken closed his eyes. "Take...take them off," he urged.

From the rustling sounds, he surmised she was stripping. His mind whirled, wondering what this woman who called herself Georgia looked like. Was she redheaded? A brunette? Blonde? Brown eyes? Blue? Hazel? Long hair? Short? Sections of his fantasy woman clicked into place like the tiles in a vertical slot machine. Long, dark hair, blue eyes, a great smile, curvy. And peeling off her clothes.

"They're off."

Ken bit his tongue to keep from asking more questions that might end the phone call. His hand slid beneath the sheet, and he imagined Georgia easing into the bed next to him.

"It's hot over here," she continued, much to his relief. "And I just couldn't sleep after leaving the club. All that nudity affected me."

She was a stripper? That explained the stage name.

His conscience eased somewhat. At least she wasn't some innocent lady shedding her modesty for the first time. And she must have an incredible body. Her shadow of an accent didn't belong to a Southern belle, but in his mind, Georgia was as lush and sticky-sweet as her name implied.

"I need to relax," she said, sighing.

Ken could almost feel her breath warming his neck. His answer was a low groan of encouragement.

"Lately I've been hoping we could become more...intimate."

"I never knew," he replied in a low tone. *The truth.*

"We've both been a little shy, but somehow, it's easier to talk about my fantasies on the phone like this."

A hot flush traveled over his skin. "Go on."

"My breasts," she said, her voice suddenly tentative again.

Round? High? Firm?

"Sensitive. *So* sensitive."

Not as visual, but he could make it work. "Mmm-hmm."

She was breathing harder now. "My hair is down and tickling my breasts."

Thank you, thank you, thank you.

"Can you picture me lying next to you?"

Could he? "Uh-huh." She was killing him. Moonlight streamed through a window next to his bed, transforming the tangled sheets into a woman's figure. Her skin was smooth and golden with faint and minuscule tan lines. Beautiful. Their hands tangled as they stroked and caressed each other.

"Touch me lower," she murmured.

His breath caught in his chest.

"Lower," she urged, and he moaned, picturing the dip of her navel and the tangle of dark hair in the vee of her thighs.

"There," she moaned, gratified. "Yes, there."

Ken tensed, moved by the emotion in her voice. "I can't wait much longer."

She was practically panting now. "Yes...now."

He imagined himself ready over her waiting body. Their moans would mingle at the union. She would close around him as he sank deeper and deeper in her warmth.

Her voice reverberated in his head, a stream of soft moans, punctuated with throaty inflection to capture a rhythm he matched without hesitation. He could never tire of her voice. "Talk to me," he begged.

"S-so...good...ohhhhhhhhh...harder...faster..."

Ken obliged, his breathing becoming more ragged with every thrust. "When you're ready," he whispered, "take me with you."

"Yes," she gasped. "Together...now...oh, yes..."

Ken's eyes rolled back as he joined her powerful release. Their voices culminated in staccato cries, then gentled to quiet moans. Satisfied sighs hummed on the line as they both labored to control their breathing.

"That...was...great," he managed between great mouthfuls of air. His body spasmed with residual pleasure and he felt utterly drained.

"Mmm-hmm," she agreed with a silky laugh, then cleared her throat. "I...guess I'd better let you get back to sleep." She'd retreated into shyness. "Good night,

Rob. Call me tomorrow." He heard a faint click, then a dial tone.

Ken floundered to sit up and managed to knock the phone and other clutter off the nightstand. He swung his feet to the floor, his heart still recovering from his unexpectedly naughty phone call. He'd seen, done, and heard a lot of things during his years as a beat cop, but this was a first. Unbeknownst to her, the woman had performed a public service.

Today—no, yesterday—had been one of the lousiest days he could remember. No deaths, thank goodness, but he'd answered an excessive number of domestic violence calls, and the criminals seemed to get younger all the time. He became a cop partly because he wanted to pass a safer world on to his nieces and nephews, and partly because he felt law enforcement was the best possible use of his God-given physical strength and mental discipline. He'd simply underestimated the sheer malice with which people treated one another, especially members of their own family.

Every cop experienced times when he simply didn't want to get up and go to work, and Ken had been entertaining such thoughts when he lay down. And although his body now tingled with muscle fatigue, his spirit sang with new vitality. Ken decided he needed to get his priorities in order and find a good woman, then maybe he wouldn't dwell on the misery he encountered every day.

And maybe he wouldn't be tempted to steal an orgasm meant for another man.

His conscience poked at him, but what could he do now? Nothing, he decided hastily, rising and striding toward the bathroom. Chalk up the misdirected phone call as a once-in-a-lifetime experience and let it be. Tomorrow, Georgia and Rob—whoever they were—would have a big laugh when they realized she'd coaxed a wrong number to climax.

Ken leaned against the sink and ran a hand through his flattened hair, thinking about the sometimes shy voice of his unwitting partner. What if, instead, she felt humiliated and kept her secret? What if she worried about the identity of the person with whom she'd shared such an intimate experience?

Nah.

He splashed his face with handfuls of cool water, then stumbled back to bed, unable to stop a slow grin and a wide yawn as he fell onto his pillow. One thing he did know. His insomnia was cured for tonight.

4

"SO HOW DID IT GO?"

Georgia jumped at the sound of Toni's voice over her shoulder, then smiled sheepishly at her friend. In fact, despite a slight headache and sitting on gum stuck to the bus seat this morning, she'd been gloating ever since her alarm had sounded. She was officially a naughty girl. Life was good.

Toni snapped her fingers in rapid succession. "Come on, you were humming, for Pete's sake."

Georgia glanced at the charts she was working on, then checked her watch. "I'm due a break. Want to get some coffee?"

"Sure."

After letting the admissions clerk know she'd be away for ten minutes, Georgia wrote "break" beside her name on a dry eraser board. "How are things in the nursery?"

Toni looked heavenward. "Please tell me what possessed me to transfer up to the fourth floor."

"You love babies, and you have the hots for the new head of obstetrics."

Her friend frowned. "Oh, yeah."

"And how's that little ploy going, by the way?"

"Well, he calls me 'Terri.'"

"Oh." Georgia hid her smile and led the way into

the staff vending room. Two med students sat at a corner table, one studying, one asleep sitting up.

Toni threw up her hands. "My question is, how did the man get through anatomy if he can't remember names?"

Georgia poured them both a paper cup of coffee, then handed Toni a packet of sugar. "He'll come around."

"I hope so. I was planning to have snared a doctor by now. No offense, Georgia—I'm not as enamored with the nursing profession as you are. I'm here to get a husband. A rich husband with talented hands."

Georgia laughed. "Liar. You're a good nurse, Toni. By the way, how was Stacey feeling this morning?"

"Not so good, but she'll recover." After glancing at the med students, she leaned forward. "So I'm dying here. Did you call Rob and...you know?"

Feeling a blush climb her neck, Georgia blew into her cup.

"What, what, *what?*"

"Yes."

Toni squealed. "I knew you could do it if you just let go. Did he like it?"

She pursed her lips, reliving flashes of last night's erotic conversation that still sent stabs of desire to her stomach. His responses had been unexpectedly enthusiastic and sensual—a side of him she'd never seen but had hoped for. "I think so." She lowered her voice and added, "It was fabulous."

Toni grinned. "You vamp, you."

Basking in her awakening, Georgia lifted her chin and smiled. She'd misbehaved and she hadn't been struck by lightning. She hadn't grown horns. And she hadn't been tempted to ogle strange men on the bus this morning. She had her unfettered hormones perfectly under control.

"I take back what I said about Rob being a bore. The man's obviously a sleeper."

"A sleeper?"

"You know, unassuming. Awakens unexpectedly." Toni wagged her eyebrows.

"Ah."

"When will you see him again?"

"I told him to call me today."

Slurping her coffee, Toni said, "Let's hope he didn't get all Republican at the light of day."

Georgia's smile fizzled. "What do you mean?"

Toni crinkled her nose and pulled an innocent face. "Nothing."

"Oh, no, what do you mean?"

A sigh escaped her friend. "The whole buyer's remorse thing. I just wondered if it was the same with phone sex as it is with real sex. You lose one out of three guys to morning-after malady, you know."

Doubts crowded her previous good cheer. "You mean you think he enjoyed it last night, but he doesn't respect me this morning?"

Toni tossed her half-empty cup into the trash can and wiped her hands together in a "that's that" motion. "Forget I said anything."

She frowned. "I'll try."

"When do you get off?" Then she winked and poked Georgia in the ribs. "*Again?*"

"Oh, you're a riot. I clock out at three."

"Don't worry, he'll call. Ta ta."

Georgia pushed aside her nagging concern and threw herself into the chaos of the afternoon. But every E.R. triage nurse typically experienced at least one day a week during which she questioned her decision to become a nurse in the first place, and today turned out to be hers. Her adolescent dreams of fixing people's bodies—and, thus, their souls—seemed ludicrous in the wake of stomach flus, food poisonings, puncture wounds and other less palatable ailments. No dramatic lifesaving procedures today. She blamed the heat for the elevated tempers. Every patient tested her patience, bickering about the wait, second-guessing the treatments she offered. As her shift progressed, Georgia's anxiety level increased. And as her anxiety level increased, her confidence waned. And as her confidence waned, she felt less and less good about her recent foray into the world of the sexually assertive.

What if Toni were right and Rob had decided her forwardness was uncouth? How would she be able to face him? She'd whipped up a little fudge sauce for their plain vanilla relationship, but had it been too rich for his blood? Since his consulting assignments required that he travel, and due to the nature of her job, they rarely spoke during the day. But after she clocked out, she'd make an exception and call him to gauge his reaction.

"What kind of a nurse are you?" a big, unpleasant-smelling man demanded when she refused to give him a physical for his medical insurance.

Georgia put her hands on her hips. "Sir, this is an emergency room, not your family doctor's office."

"I don't have a family doctor. That's why I came here. I figured it would be faster."

"Get out," she said, jerking her thumb toward the door. "You're taking up room for people who have legitimate emergencies."

Her statement really wasn't true, at least not today, she noted with an irritated grunt as the man stalked out. Almost every person who came through the door had made a mockery of E.R. medicine, a mockery of her childhood aspirations. She woke up every morning, eager to aid those in need, eager to make a real difference in someone's life. But even Nurse Goody-Two-Shoes had her limits. God help the next person who came in to waste her time and the hospital's resources, because she certainly wouldn't.

"WHISTLING? Man, you must've gotten lucky last night."

Unwrapping a hamburger on his knee, since every square inch of his desk was occupied, Ken cut his gaze toward his partner. "Get your mind out of the gutter, Klone. I slept well, that's all. Damn near forgot what it was like."

The older man grinned and proceeded to talk with his mouth full of club sandwich. "What, no hot number to keep you up all night?"

A *wrong* hot number. "Man, you ask too many questions."

"Job hazard," Klone said, undaunted. "You've been complaining about your insomnia for weeks, but I think you've just been up late womanizing and partying."

"Yeah, my life isn't half as interesting as you lead people to believe."

"Well, then maybe you've been moonlighting."

"Klone, I haven't been moonlighting." Unless he could get paid for working crossword puzzles in the wee hours of the morning.

"Because if you need some extra cash to fund your lifestyle, every business in town is clamoring for cops to direct traffic on their off-hours. If you ask me, the city needs to put up a few more stoplights. Where are you working?"

"Klone, I have not been moonlighting."

"Well, if you ask me, it's high time you find a good woman to settle down with."

"I didn't ask you."

"That's why you're not sleeping, because you're yearning for a soul mate."

Ken grimaced and looked around at their colleagues moving about. "Jesus, keep your voice down. Have you been reading *Cosmo* or something?" He grunted. "I've told you before, marriage isn't for me." He wanted his mind squarely on his job. His first partner out of the academy had been a good-natured fellow, top of his class, with a successful career ahead of him until he met his "soul mate," a woman who messed with his mind so badly, he'd committed grievous errors on the job. The last time Ken had seen him, the guy was unemployed, divorced, and a tad on the bitter side.

Ken's own experiences were somewhat less dramatic, but he'd tired of vapid women who seemed determined to worm their way into his life regardless of his feelings on the matter. Although he was larger than the average man, he was brighter than most women gave him credit for. Relationships in general were a giant hassle. Last night was the first time he'd had sex with a woman without worrying about whether potpourri would suddenly appear in his bathroom.

Klone took another bite. "All I'm saying is that with a stressful job like this, you need a warm body to go home to every night. Someone to remind you that everyone in this world ain't a criminal. Eighteen years now and Louise and me still do the deed every Friday night during *The Tonight Show*. Well, except for the two times she was in the hospital after the kids were born."

Ken was forced to listen while he chewed the overdone burger, then he swallowed. "I can't tell you how much I didn't want to hear that. And don't talk with your mouth full, for Crissake."

Klone made a perfunctory swipe at his mouth with a wadded-up paper napkin. "I'm just concerned about what you're doing with your life. You don't have to get all aggravated."

Immediately contrite, Ken ground his teeth, then said, "Klone, I *like* being single."

His partner shook his head and expelled a grave sigh. "Son, someday you're gonna learn the hard way that we can't always have things the way we like them."

Ken banked the half-eaten burger into a trash can,

trying to block out the voice of Georgia the mysterious phone seductress. *I'm not wearing panties.* That, he liked. "Where does the Fleming burglary case stand?"

Klone shifted in his seat, oblivious to Ken's strategy to change the subject. He held up a smudged piece of paper with a dollop of mayonnaise on the corner. "I got a tip to check out a pawnshop for some of the missing jewelry."

Ken took the piece of paper, heedful of the mayonnaise and his navy uniform shirt, then pushed himself to his feet. "I'll look into it."

Klone half stood. "You want some company?"

"No, I volunteered to pull truancy duty at the mall this afternoon, and this place is on the way."

His partner made a face. "Better you pulling truancy than me."

"My good deed for the week," Ken agreed wryly. "Catch you later." On the way out of the station, he stopped by the locker room to brush his teeth. The small square mirror reflected sharp cheekbones—probably due to his lousy appetite of late—and his dark hair seemed more unruly than ever, despite his efforts to keep the length short enough to curtail the curl. Damned humidity.

But for once, his dark eyes weren't red-rimmed, and his neck didn't have a crick in it. His persistent insomnia had affected him more than he'd realized, leaving him restless and irritable and susceptible to behavior in which he wouldn't normally indulge.

Such as pretending to be the deserving boyfriend of a woman who was more passionate than anyone he'd ever dated.

He banged his locker door closed, then exited to the parking garage, whistling tunelessly in an attempt to stop himself from thinking about how he caould find the woman on the phone. After swinging into his squad car, he checked the dash equipment, then started the engine and pulled out onto a side street. No sir, he wasn't about to consider ways he could use the resources at his disposal to find out who she was.

Like checking the dozen or so strip joints for a dancer named Georgia.

Like performing a computer search on the city directory database for female residents named Georgia.

Like checking his own phone records to see from where the call had originated.

He thumped the steering wheel in frustration, hating himself for allowing the unknown caller to get under his skin. It was no big deal, he told himself as he wheeled into the parking lot of the pawnshop. Because the woman was nobody to him and probably wouldn't give the incident much thought even after she discovered the blunder. And because the woman was a nymphette who had more interesting things going on in her life than worrying about the schmuck who had filched a freebie. No, he really shouldn't be concerned that the woman might be disturbed when she realized her mistake.

So, why was he?

With much effort, Ken blocked out the voice of the seductive caller to take care of the tasks at hand. The stop into the pawnshop proved to be fruitful. Based on the written descriptions from the burglarized homeowner, he recovered two rings and a bracelet, along with the bad Polaroid photo of the woman who had pawned the pieces. He locked the bagged articles in the trunk of his car, then slid behind the steering wheel, suddenly looking forward to truancy duty, despite the smart mouths of the hooky-playing teens he would inevitably find walking the corridors of the mall and hanging out in the parking lot. Kids could be puzzling these days, but he had a good motivator— the memory of the cop who had routed his own behind out of an arcade twenty years ago and harassed him back into high school.

Ken eased into fast-moving traffic—drivers were always willing to let a police car merge—then turned in the direction of the mall. Out of the corner of his eye, Ken saw a small figure dart into the street directly in his path. His heart vaulted to his throat as he slammed on the brake so hard he was sure he would trigger a pileup. A sickening thunk sounded as his front left bumper made contact with a yielding body. Horns blasted all around him. Miraculously, the truck behind him stopped with no impact. Immediately Ken flipped on the blue lights, then sprang from his seat, praying every step of the way.

Fear nearly paralyzed him when he saw blood on his car and the lifeless form on the street. Two seconds later his knees weakened with relief that he hadn't hit a child. Still, the sight of the large dog lying beneath his bumper put a stone in his stomach. His hands shook slightly as he touched the animal to see if it was alive.

It was. Although he didn't know much about dogs, this one appeared to be a mutt. Multicolored long hair covered its body, although its face was broad and blunt. He wore no collar. When Ken stroked its back, the dog opened his eyes and whined, then tried to stand, only to collapse, emitting painful little barks.

"Sorry, boy," he murmured, aware of a crowd gathering around. One of the dog's legs bent at an odd angle, and he was bleeding badly from the hip. Gathering his wits, Ken looked around and spied the entrance to the County Hospital emergency room less than a half block away. Perhaps someone there could at least stop the bleeding until he could transport the dog to a veterinary clinic.

Decision made, he tied a handkerchief around the dog's muzzle to keep him from biting in his pain, then bundled the dog into the back seat of his squad car. He covered its trembling form with a blanket from the trunk, knowing the gesture probably gave him more comfort that it gave the dog. He hoped against hope he hadn't mortally wounded the poor pooch. Ken slid into his seat, and zeroed in on the emergency room entrance. He'd find help there.

5

"SEE YOU TOMORROW," Georgia called to a co-worker as she walked toward the E.R. exit.

What a ghastly day. She removed her name badge and her pace quickened at the thought of talking to Rob. After mulling the matter for hours, she'd decided that he couldn't have feigned his responses last night. She knew abandon when she heard it, and he'd had it in spades. He'd probably already left her a message at home.

The service door next to the stairs burst open and a tall uniformed police officer emerged carrying a small body wrapped in a blanket. "He ran in front of my car," he said, his chest heaving. "He's bleeding, and I think his leg is broken."

Adrenaline and years of training took over and she bolted into action, waving him toward a triage room and yelling ahead as she jogged beside him. "We have a small victim who was struck by a car! Which room is available?"

"Three," the clerk said, handing her a chart as she passed. People parted and Georgia looked for the attending doctor as she led the way into the empty room. "Somebody get Dr. Story," she called before the door closed, then automatically grabbed a pair of surgical gloves from an overflowing box.

She felt a split second of sympathy for the broad-shouldered police officer who lowered his bundle gently onto the examining table. His shirt was blood-stained and his face was creased with worry that pulled at her heart. *This* was the basis of E.R. medicine. *This* was how she could make a difference in the world. She felt an instant bond with the man. He, too, was in the business of saving lives.

"Do you have the victim's name?" she asked, stepping forward.

"No," the officer said, then pulled back the blanket. "He wasn't wearing a collar."

Georgia froze as she surveyed the hairy mass. "It's a dog."

"Yes, ma'am."

His Southern manners aside, exasperation puffed her cheeks as the bond between them vanished with a poof. She stripped off the surgical gloves and strove to keep her voice even. "We treat people here, Officer, not animals."

He frowned. "Can't you make an exception?"

"Absolutely," she said ruefully, "if I wanted to lose my job." She stepped to the door and yelled, "Cancel the call for Dr. Story." Turning back to the dark-haired policeman, she pulled her most professional face. "We have health codes to maintain. You, of all people, should know that."

His dark eyebrows knitted and he adopted a wide-legged stance. "You could at least bandage the cut."

Her heart went out to the poor dog, and she crossed her arms to keep from following her instincts to heal. She also had instincts to eat, pay rent and not default on school loans, which would be difficult to satisfy if she were fired. Even after a year, she was still considered a greenhorn in emergency medicine. Dr. Story watched her like a hawk. A flagrant violation like this one could be the end of her career at County Hospital, a stain on her record. Georgia swallowed and averted her gaze. "I'm sorry—hospital procedures. The veterinary clinic on Sixteenth Street is the closest facility."

The officer's anger was palpable. But instead of leaving, he turned and scanned the shelves of supplies, his big hands touching everything.

"What are you doing?"

"What *you* should be doing," he growled, then yanked a roll of gauze from a box and unrolled several lengths.

She opened her mouth to protest, then realized the futility of arguing with a man twice her size, with three times the determination. Georgia hung back, but as he clumsily wrapped the gauze around the dog's body, something...happened. Unexpected warmth and admiration expanded her chest. The man hadn't a clue what to do, but was driven to act. However misguided, she couldn't help but respect his zeal. When he unwound another twenty feet or so of the gauze, she shook her head. Just like a man to overdo.

"That's enough," she said quietly.

He glanced up, his eyes flashing, ready for battle.

"He won't be able to breathe," she added, then donned more gloves and found tape and scissors. With resignation that she'd probably get written up and reprimanded, if not out-and-out fired, Georgia leaned forward and finished the bandaging, then gave the animal a perfunctory examination. The dog and the cop were wide-eyed and silent, but she could feel the man's anger had dissipated. "Officer—?"

"Medlock," he supplied.

"Officer Medlock, my knowledge of a dog's anatomy is limited, but it appears he does indeed have a broken leg. He might have a broken rib or two as well, but his breathing is good, so I don't believe his lungs were punctured. There's no blood in the mouth, nose, or ears, so if he has internal bleeding, it does not seem to be profuse. And that—" she stepped back and peeled off her gloves "—is absolutely all I can do."

He smiled suddenly and her breath caught in appreciation. Officer Medlock was a great-looking man. Pushy, but great-looking. When she realized she was staring, embarrassment swept over her. Her appreciation of his masculinity was stirred only because of her state of...stirredness.

"Thank you, Dr.—?"

"I'm an R.N.," she said. "Nurse Adams."

"Nurse Adams," he repeated. "Thank you for giving me peace of mind, ma'am."

Her pulse kicked higher under his scrutiny. Few, if any, grown men called her "ma'am." It was kind of...pleasurable. "You're welcome. Now please get out of here while I still have a job."

Ken tried to study the woman's face without appearing to. Her dark blue eyes were heavy-lidded and astonishing, and her mouth... The woman had that fresh-faced, girl-next-door vitality that provoked neighboring boys to buy binoculars. He mentally shook himself, realizing that last night's incognito phone call was behind his heightened awareness. The dog whined, reminding him of his immediate priority. Gently, he rewrapped the animal and lifted the bundle from the table.

The nurse held open the door. "I was just going off duty," she said with the barest hint of a smile. "I'll show you the exit."

"To guarantee I make it out of here?" he asked wryly.

"Something like that."

As he laughed good-naturedly, she removed a leather shoulder bag from behind a counter, then told a clerk she was leaving and ordered an immediate disinfecting of exam room three. As she joined him, he was overwhelmed with the urge to know her, to find out if she were involved with anyone. He scoffed inwardly. Of course someone as beautiful as she would already be involved, maybe married, and probably to a doctor who earned ten times as much as a policeman. Ken tried to keep the dog's head covered as they headed toward the exit so he wouldn't get the woman into trouble, but the poor mutt whined most of the way, raising eyebrows. His unwilling cohort kept her eyes averted and walked swiftly.

"Georgia!"

At the sound of the name that had been on the periphery of his brain all day, Ken halted midstride. The woman next to him hesitated, then kept going.

"Georgia!" someone repeated, louder. He turned to see a plump woman jogging toward them. The comely nurse turned as well.

Ken's feet stopped moving as his brain tried to assimilate the information. This woman's name was Georgia? He'd never met anyone named Georgia. What were the chances he'd meet two in less than twenty-four hours? He zeroed in on her voice and tried to match hers with the one running through his head. It was possible—he almost laughed—but highly unlikely.

Still, his mind raced for a logical-sounding question that might help him determine if this fabulous-looking woman was the same... No, she simply couldn't be.

"Get out of here," she hissed out of the side of her mouth.

But his feet refused to move.

"Georgia," the woman gasped, lumbering to a halt in front of them. Then she zeroed in on the whining blanket. "Is that a *dog?*"

"Melanie, did you need something?" Nurse Adams asked her, while frowning at him and nodding toward the exit.

The other woman craned her neck, eyes alight with curiosity, then handed his companion a yellow sticky-note. "I almost forgot to give you this message. Rob phoned and said he was called out of town unexpectedly."

Ken swallowed and nearly dropped his patient. *Rob?*

6

His tongue had turned to cotton. Ken stared at the woman he'd just met as she read the note in her hand. *This* gorgeous woman was the same silky-throated creature who had roused him from sleep last night? His skin tingled with revelation. He glanced up, expecting a spotlight to be shining on his guilt-ridden head.

"Thank you, Melanie," she said tersely, then proceeded through the door, seemingly lost in thought.

But Ken wasn't ready to let Nurse Georgia Adams walk out of his life. He hurried forward, mindful of the bundle in his arms. "Wait!"

She turned back, but seemed less than thrilled to see him still standing there. "As I said, Officer, the vet clinic is on Sixteenth Street. You don't need an appointment."

He tilted his head, desperate to extend their conversation. "D-don't I know you from somewhere?"

She looked perplexed. "I don't think so. I've never been in trouble with the police."

"Georgia Adams," he murmured to himself, pretending to mull her identity, when in truth, he simply liked the way her name rolled off his tongue. "Georgia Adams..."

"Maybe you've seen me in the halls of the hospital," she offered.

"Wait a minute," he said, improvising. "I know a guy named Rob who dates a woman named Georgia."

She took a half step toward him. "Rob Trainer?"

Ah, the identity of the unwittingly deprived boyfriend. "Um, yes." He shifted the dog's weight to his left side while he extended his right hand. "Ken Medlock."

She hesitated, then placed her soft, healing hand in his. "How do you do, Officer Medlock."

"Ken is fine," he said, reluctantly releasing her hand.

"I'll tell Rob I ran into you when he returns from his business trip."

Uh-oh. "Well, he might not remember me—I've only spoken to him a couple of times...casually." He swallowed. "At the gym?"

"The gym on Arrow Street? Yes, that's where Rob works out." She stroked the dog's ear where the blanket had fallen away. "Poor boy, I hope he's okay."

He could only nod, struck dumb by the serendipity that had brought them together. He wasn't the superstitious type, but it had to be some sort of sign...didn't it?

"Well," she said, lifting her hand in a little wave, "good luck. I'm sure the clinic will fix up your friend like new."

She pivoted on the heels of her sensible white shoes, dragging off a white lab coat to reveal pink scrubs...and a fabulous figure. Her dark hair was pulled into a clasp at the nape of her neck, hanging midway to her back. Nurse Georgia Adams walked thirty feet away to a bus stop, then settled herself onto a wooden bench to wait, just as if she weren't the most beautiful woman on the streets of Birmingham.

Then Ken smiled as a snatch of their conversation returned to him. *I'll tell Rob I ran into you when he returns from his business trip.*

The most beautiful woman on the streets of Birmingham was alone for a few days.

The dog whimpered, yanking his good sense back from the gates of Fantasyland. Ken hurried toward his squad car.

GEORGIA SHIFTED on the hard bench, her cheeks burning with shame. Since Rob had opted to leave her a message at the hospital instead of talking to her in person, he must be upset over their little "session." Toni was right; she'd spooked him by being so forward. She read the note again, wishing the hastily scribbled message had divulged where he was going, or even how long he'd be gone. *Called out of town unexpectedly. Rob.*

The man's communication was nothing if not...economical. But Stacey's wedding was only three days away, and she'd been looking forward to attending it with Rob in the hope that witnessing someone else's lifetime commitment would shed some light on their own aimless path.

She turned her head and watched Officer Ken Medlock's broad back receding. He still held the injured dog in his arms, and when a corner of the blanket fell, he tucked it back in place. Georgia smiled, thinking how few men would have taken the time to aid a wounded animal, especially a big, strapping man. She'd been surprised to hear that he knew Rob. Officer Ken seemed more...earthy...than Rob's yuppie accountant friends. Of course, he did say they only knew each other from the gym. She frowned just as he rounded the corner and disappeared from view. On the other hand, they must be more than mere acquaintances if Rob had mentioned her name.

Georgia bit into her lower lip, realizing she'd never thought about the kinds of things Rob might say about her to his friends. Would he tell them about the phone sex? She had told Toni, but only because Toni had encouraged her to share her fantasies with Rob in the first place. And she trusted Toni as a confidante.

But the idea of Rob's friends knowing made her extremely uneasy. Almost as uneasy as the fact that she didn't know whether Rob would tell them.

In truth, she really didn't know that much about the habits and acquaintances of the man whom she'd met at the party of a friend of a friend going on ten months ago. They had met over soggy egg rolls and talked about a movie they'd both seen and hated. She hadn't been bowled over, but he was nice and seemed nonpsychotic—a definite bonus in today's singles market.

When Rob Trainer had called a week later to invite her to a Chamber of Commerce cocktail party, she'd said yes, and they'd been seeing each other regularly since. Hectic schedules on both their parts had minimized their dating time to scant weekends and occasional day trips out of Birmingham. Yet even when they were together, Rob wasn't a chatty fellow. His

parents were from Cincinnati, but now that she
thought about it, she couldn't remember if he'd ever
mentioned siblings.

But still waters ran deep. Rob was a handsome,
pleasant man with enough ambition for three people.
So what if he wasn't always thoughtful and romantic—what man was? An unbidden image of Officer
Ken's anxious expression over the injured dog pulled
at her heart. Was Rob an animal lover? She doubted it,
considering what a neatnik he was. But in her musings, she was starting to realize how few personal details she knew about the man with whom she had ini-
tiated phone sex. For all she knew, he could be a serial
killer with a low sex drive. Maybe *that* was why he
was to familiar Officer Ken.

Then she scoffed at her own silliness. For a straight-
laced guy like Rob, a mere parking citation would be
tantamount to a public flogging. Rob hadn't been
quite as forthcoming with his background as she'd
been with hers, but one thing she did know about her
boyfriend—he was by the book.

Er, excluding *The Joy of Sex*, that is.

A staccato honk pulled her gaze from the spot she'd
last seen the attractive police officer. The bus driver
glared at her through the open door. "You comin' or
not, lady?"

Georgia jumped to her feet and bounded aboard. If
she didn't stop daydreaming, she'd never finish her
errands. But even squeezing into a crowded seat
among noisy passengers couldn't distract her from the
recollection of Ken Medlock's rugged frame. Were
Rob's shoulders that wide? She might stop locking her

doors if every Birmingham police officer evoked that kind of security.

With a rueful sigh, she acknowledged the only reason she had responded physically to the uniformed man was that her late-night session with Rob had awakened disobedient places within her. Places that—dwelled upon for mere seconds, like now—sprang to life. Her thighs tingled, her breasts tightened, her stomach clenched. Her gaze remained fixed on the back of the seat in front of her. Her focus blurred, and external noises diminished to a static buzz.

Slices of their chance encounter jumped into her brain randomly, like a trailer to a movie. His square jawline, his broad nose, his sincere eyes. *Nurse Adams, thank you for giving me peace of mind.* His smile, his gratitude for her assistance. *D-don't I know you from somewhere?*

Had he felt it too—a connection? An electric physical attraction born of proximity and a common goal?

She admonished herself for thinking sexy thoughts about a man she just met, but something about Officer Ken Medlock seemed familiar. Or maybe his all-American robust good looks just made him seem approachable, as if he were someone she *should* know—like a handsome man in a magazine ad whose eyes reached out to a woman, telling her she was special and if only he could walk off the page, he would make her his. It could happen.

"Town Center Mall!" the driver shouted, yanking her from her schoolgirl fantasies. Georgia disembarked slowly, still suffering from the surreal effects of her musings, and headed in the direction of a shop

Toni had recommended to buy a dress for Stacey's wedding. Her friend had described the clothes at Latest & Greatest as "cool duds on the cheap" and insisted Georgia ask for Tom Tom.

But Tom Tom, as it turned out, was *two* men, both named Tom, who were apparently unrelated, yet spoke in tandem.

"Ah, Toni sent you! We have—"

"—exactly what you need for a—"

"—summer afternoon wedding. Won't you—"

"—follow us?"

Georgia's gaze bounced back and forth, then she nodded and followed them to a rack of long filmy dresses. They flipped through the hangers, each whipping out a flowing garment.

"The pink stripe will be beautiful—"

"—with your hair. But the yellow—"

"—will set off your lovely—"

"—complexion. Although the blue floral—"

"—is a perfect complement for your eyes." The men looked at each other, then nodded and said in unison, "The blue floral."

Not her first choice, Georgia acknowledged silently. In fact, floral prints didn't even make her short list; she gravitated to solid-colored clothing. But since her opinion obviously didn't matter, she mutely acquiesced as they shooed her into a dressing room and waited outside, the toes of their pointy shoes tapping. To her surprise, they were right—the blue floral mimicked the indigo of her eyes, and the voluminous fabric fell in feminine folds that skimmed her ankles.

She smiled into the mirror, turning quickly to watch

the delicate hem float on the air. Suddenly, her older sister Fannie came to mind. Georgia had always tagged along to stores and sat in a corner of the dressing room to watch the magical Fannie try on dress after dress for the many dances and parties she attended. She was breathtaking, and possessed an uncanny knack for picking the dress that best showed off her perfect skin and more perfect figure. Their mother would stand behind Fannie in the mirror, beaming as the saleswomen proclaimed Fannie the most beautiful girl they'd ever seen. No one could take their eyes off her, most especially their mother, from whom Fannie had inherited her flashing green eyes and glossy flaxen hair.

Meanwhile, Georgia, being her father's namesake and sporting her father's blue eyes and unremarkable brownish hair, withdrew more and more into the background. Once they'd even left her at a department store by accident. Her father, whom she adored, had come to pick her up and had stopped at a pawnshop on the way home to buy a used 35mm camera. Georgia had been hooked instantly. Photography became her escape, her window on the human condition, and a link to her beloved father. He had died from cancer the summer she turned sixteen. She had just learned to drive, she recalled. Funny, but to this day, she'd never gotten her driver's license.

Her mother loved her; she had simply been preoccupied with Fannie and all that Fannie was. She still was, except now the preoccupation included Fannie's wealthy husband and their two darling daughters. It was a full-time job for her mother, keeping up with the accoutrements of Fannie's charmed life in Denver. Georgia had been left to her own devices, furthering her photography and attending nursing school. One didn't have to be spectacular looking or musically inclined or a prima ballerina to take pictures, or to be a nurse.

Georgia scrutinized her silhouette and frowned. A darn good thing, too.

"How's it going in there?" one of the Toms called.

She exhaled and emerged nervously to head-nodding and hmm-hmming.

"Darling, you will—"

"—upstage the bride."

She smiled, pleased despite their exaggeration. Then, feeling somewhat like a dressmaker's dummy, she submitted to their tucking and pinning to the tune of snapped fingers and quick sniffs.

"What will your date be wearing?" the taller one asked.

"A suit, I suppose," she said. If he came, that is.

"A *navy* suit?" the other one asked, his voice suspicious. "He simply must wear navy to complement your dress."

She nodded mutely. Being a nice dresser, Rob probably had a navy suit in his closet. Georgia frowned. But why did the image of a navy uniform keep popping into her mind?

Both Toms scribbled on a piece of paper. "Go to the accessories department in Elm's and buy the Derrin straw hat—"

"—with a white band. Then go to footwear and buy the white espadrilles—"

"—with the ankle strap. By the time you get back—"

"—your lovely frock will be ready."

They smiled in unison and recapped their ink pens. Powerless to disagree in the wake of their frighteningly good taste, she took the piece of paper and stopped herself short of a curtsey before she redonned her scrubs and left the store. Mall merchandising, she suddenly noticed, was all about sex. Loud, pulsing music. Lingerie and skimpy clothing in the windows. Judging from their stiff nipples, even the mannequins were turned on.

Bombarded with erotic cues, she simply couldn't stop thinking about the phone call. And she couldn't stop obsessing over Rob's reaction. Darn Toni for raising the questions in the first place. And darn that Ken Medlock for forcing his way into her impossibly crowded mind. She was suddenly glad she would most likely never see the man again.

As she was told, Georgia headed toward Elm's and, unfamiliar with the upscale store, meandered around until she found the accessories department. Feeling somewhat conspicuous, she glanced all around before trying on hats in the line the men had suggested. *Which* Derrin straw hat with a white band? There were so many. She tried on style after style, then conceded she hadn't enjoyed herself so much in a long time. She even loosened the clasp from her hair, toying with the idea of wearing it down for the wedding. At last she settled on a bowler style, crossing her fingers that Tom Tom wouldn't object to her choice. The espadrilles were fun and comfortable, but a whole heck of a lot more expensive now than when they were first popular a couple of decades ago.

Swinging both bags, she gave in to the rumbling in her stomach and stopped at the food court for a bagel and cream cheese. The mall was a great place to people-watch, a favorite pastime, even without her camera. Take that old man over there reading the paper—priceless. Or the triplets in the combination stroller, all eating ice cream. Or the policeman leaned over, lecturing a group of preteens seated around a table.

Georgia stopped chewing and squinted. Officer Medlock? Her pulse kicked up. What was he doing here at the mall? She watched him send the kids on their way, then glanced at her watch. Ah, the kids were playing hooky. He stood with his hands on his hips and stared after the boys who chanced sullen looks over their shoulders while they shuffled toward the exit.

She wondered how the dog had fared, and decided it was perfectly legitimate for her to ask—she'd put her job on the line, after all. But while she watched, a young woman tottered up to him wearing painted-on clothing, high heels, and exhibiting her mastery of hair-toss. Georgia glanced down at her own institutional clothing and resolved to slink out unnoticed. The officer responded to the young woman's inquiry with a smile that made Georgia swallow a chunk of bagel without chewing.

It promptly lodged in her esophagus, effectively blocking her airway. Georgia clutched her throat. She was choking. She was going to die with last night's tawdry act on her conscience... Her next conversation would be with St. Peter: "Oh, and here's Miss Ring-a-Ding-Ding..."

7

GEORGIA STOOD and flailed for a few seconds, trying to get the attention of the people around her before conceding she would have to try to administer the Heimlich maneuver on herself—perhaps on the back of a chair?

In the background she heard someone yell, "She's choking!" and before she could fling herself against a solid surface, two strong arms encircled her from behind and applied a quick upthrust below her breastbone. Her feet dangled. On the second thrust, the chunk of bread projected out of her mouth like a torpedo, bouncing off a table a few feet away. People scattered. She gasped for air like a racehorse.

Background applause registered dimly in her oxygen-deprived brain. She was shepherded into a seated position. "Are you all right?" she barely heard.

She blinked a man's face into view. An attractive man. A familiar, attractive man.

"Georgia, are you all right?"

She nodded in abject mortification, realizing that Officer Ken Medlock had saved her life. Didn't that mean he now owned her soul or something? He was kneeling before her, his face creased with the same concern she'd seen when he was carrying the dog. She felt like an idiot.

"How about something to drink?" he asked, his face close to hers.

The man had a cleft in his chin worthy of a super-hero. A strong nose, broad and straight. And she was mesmerized by his serious brown eyes, surrounded by layers of dark lashes and thick eyebrows that were, at the moment, raised. For lack of a better response, she nodded, then tried to clear her head as he reached for her drink. Her skin tingled like menthol—proba-bly because everyone was staring, certainly not be-cause of this man's proximity. She was, however, mindful of his big body. The dark blue uniform was tailor-made to form to his powerful frame.

His fingers dwarfed the paper cup he extended. Georgia noticed he wore a scholarly ring of some kind, but not the married kind.

Not that it mattered. She sipped slowly from the cup of fizzy drink, feeling his gaze bore into her and realizing she must look a fright—muss-haired, flush-faced and teary-eyed from the coughing. Her attempt at laughter came out sounding a little strangled. "You're a regular hero today, aren't you?"

His grin was boyish. "No heroes here, ma'am. Just doing my job."

His dark hair was short, but not short enough to curb the curl on top, highlighted by the sun streaming in from the skylights above them. Amazing how she hadn't known Officer Ken Medlock existed before to-day, yet their paths had crossed twice in a matter of hours.

"It's a small world, isn't it?" he asked, as if he'd read her mind. That uniform...those eyes...as if he could delve into her psyche, see all her dirty little secrets. She had yet to recover from her episode with Rob, and here she was, lusting after a virtual stranger. Just as she'd feared. Overnight, she had plunged herself into a cesspool of sexuality.

"Looks like you've been having fun up until now," he said lightly, gesturing to her Elm's shopping bags.

In her case, fun always led to misfortune. From now on, fun was her red flag: If fun, then cease and desist.

"Special occasion?" he asked, eyeing the hatbox.

The man had an amazing-looking mouth. Good for...blowing whistles. "A wedding," she croaked.

"Yours?"

From the size of his lopsided grin, he was trying to be funny. As if she couldn't possibly be the bride. Had he been chatting with her mother? She pursed her mouth, suddenly feeling cranky. "No, not mine."

He tilted his head. "Are you sure you're all right, ma'am?"

"Of course," she said, drawing back to massage her side. "That is, if you didn't crack a rib. I'm a registered nurse, Officer Medlock, perfectly capable of administering the Heimlich maneuver to myself."

He gestured vaguely to her chest area. "But you weren't doing it."

She inhaled, indignant. "I was calmly looking for a chair of the proper height."

The man appeared to be immensely amused. "Well, pardon me. Perhaps I should've just watched you turn blue while you looked for the right chair. Or better yet, maybe I should've sent you to a clinic on the other side of town."

Officer Ken was entirely too cocky. Smothering images her unfortunate choice of adjective conjured up, she stood and hurriedly cleared her ill-fated meal.

"Aren't you going to finish eating?"

"No." The two Toms were probably looking for her.

"Maybe you should have a doctor check you over."

And she needed to talk to Rob. "Officer, I think I can make that determination for myself." Georgia stooped to gather her bags and noticed the man had extremely large feet. Oi.

"I'll have to file a report on what happened here," he said. "Should I send you a copy?"

And be reminded of him again? And this spectacle? "No. Goodbye."

He inclined his head. "Ma'am."

His honeyed politeness only fueled her anxiety. She dragged her gaze from him and whirled toward the exit just in time for her conscience to kick in. With a chagrined sigh, Georgia turned back. "By the way, Officer, how's the dog?"

He crossed his arms over his chest, displacing all kinds of muscle. "The vet said he'd be fine."

"G-good," she said.

He nodded, his expression unreadable, although she got the impression he wasn't thinking about the rescued pet.

"Well...thanks."

"You're welcome, ma'am."

She didn't look back as she left the food court, but she could feel Ken Medlock's knowing gaze upon her even after she finished her errands and arrived at her apartment. Between the uniform and his massive frame, the infuriating man packed a powerful punch of sex appeal.

It was a good thing he was so irritating and she was so...fulfilled. Yes, fulfilled.

When she saw the light flashing on her new message recorder, her heartbeat raced. *Rob.* What would he say? Was he excited by the new phase of their relationship, or had she gone too far? After a deep breath, she pushed the Play button, then jumped when a mechanical voice blasted into the stale air of her apartment.

"Thank you for buying this Temeteck product! This is a test message to allow you to adjust the volume. Press '1' if you don't want this message to play again."

Georgia frowned and stabbed the "1" button. Darn it. Oh, well, it was still early. Rob would probably call later. She grabbed a bottle of water and the mail where she'd left it on the table and settled as best she could onto her hard sofa, which she was starting to despise.

Bills, bills, and a letter from her mother. Georgia winced, but decided to get it over with. She slid her finger under the envelope flap, then removed the two pages covered with her mother's familiar script. Same old, same old. She was extending her visit in Denver with Fannie and Fannie's perfect family unit. They needed her, after all.

Which meant that she didn't, of course. Georgia had been their father's child, Fannie their mother's. She didn't begrudge her sister's seemingly charmed life and abiding happiness, but she did resent her mother's implication that Georgia was less of a dutiful daughter for not producing an environment conducive to a visiting, meddling parent.

As expected, the chatty letter ended with:

P.S. I lit a candle for you at Mass on Saturday that someday you will find a man who will make you as happy as Albert makes Fannie. How is Bob?

Georgia closed her eyes and laid her head back on the couch. Fannie had made The American Dream look so easy. She'd slighted her studies in favor of socializing and snared the son of the man who'd created some newfangled racing snow ski, ergo the lodge in Denver big enough to host the winter Olympics. Their wedding had been the social event of the year in Denver. Georgia's bridesmaid gown had cost as much as a semester's tuition. And their mother... Well, *her* happiness was cinched when the star of a nationally syndicated decorating show flew in from Los Angeles just to make the table arrangements.

How was a little sister supposed to follow that act? She wanted all those wonderful things, too, but maybe Fannie had inherited all the husband-hunting genes. Maybe she was destined to be simply a good aunt.

Her phone rang, an alien noise that sounded like a sick pet. *Rob, finally.* She yanked up the portable phone and pressed the Talk button. "Hello?"

"Hey, it's me," Toni said.

"Oh, hi."

"I take it from your depressed tone that Rob hasn't yet called to, um, return the favor?"

She sighed. "He left a message at the hospital saying he was called out of town unexpectedly, and that he would phone, but I haven't heard from him yet."

"He's probably just busy or away from a phone. Hey, what's this about you treating a dog in the E.R.?"

Georgia swallowed. "How much trouble am I in?"

"A lot. What the heck happened?"

She stood and paced the room. "A cop came running in carrying a patient wrapped in a blanket. I didn't find out it was a dog until we were already in an exam room."

"So you booted out the cop, right?"

"I tried. But when I refused to treat the dog, the guy started bandaging him up himself."

"So being the big-hearted person you are, you gave him a hand."

"I didn't have a choice!"

"Uh-huh. Well, I hope the guy was worth the grief you're going to catch tomorrow."

She glowered. "He wasn't."

"Dr. Story is liable to fire you, you know."

"Thank you for giving me something else to obsess about this evening."

"Something else? Oh, you're worried about Rob's reaction."

Georgia gasped. "I was fine until you started talking about buyer's remorse!"

"Well, just in case things don't work out with Rob, is the cop single?"

"I so completely didn't ask."

"Cops are supposed to be great in bed."

She blinked away the image of the man's huge feet.

"I could have sworn we were talking about me being fired."

"Just a little trivia I thought you might be interested in."

Erotic visions skipped through her head—uniforms, frisking, handcuffs. "Well, I'm not."

"Hey, did you find a dress?"

"Yes, the Toms practically flung it on me."

"Aren't they great?"

"I think 'frightening' is the word you're looking for."

"But I'm sure you'll look fabulous for Rob at the wedding."

"I just hope he's back in time to go with me."

"Yeah, you can tell a lot about a guy by how he acts at a wedding. You're lucky that you have the chance to expose him at this point in your relationship."

Georgia sighed. "I'm not so sure that Rob and I have a relationship."

"Well, after last night, he's bound to make a move in one direction or another."

"Yeah, well, thanks again for reminding me how far out on a limb I've climbed."

"Don't worry about Rob. Just try to get to work a few minutes early tomorrow to circumvent Dr. Story's lecture. And dress up."

"I appreciate the warning. See you tomorrow."

She disconnected the call, feeling itchy and restless. What a lousy end to such a promising day. Waiting for Rob to call, the dog episode, the choking incident, her mother's letter. She laughed morosely. Her mother would never have forgiven her if she'd died at the mall—well, maybe in Nordstrom's, but certainly not in the food court.

She closed her eyes, trying to pinpoint her unease, and Ken Medlock's face came to her. Why did the stranger push her buttons? Because he challenged her authority? Because he made her feel inept? Because his intriguing presence mocked her decision to become more intimate with Rob?

Rob. Such a nice man. So...predictable. Nice and predictable. The kind of man a woman could depend on to be faithful. In these days of disposable families, fidelity and trust were high on her list of characteristics in a lasting partner. Rob never looked at other women when they were out together, and he never bragged about a colorful sexual history. He was a gentleman.

She poked her tongue into her cheek. Well, he didn't call her "ma'am" in a rolling Southern tongue, but he was a gentleman nonetheless. Georgia tried not to dwell on the fact that while Rob never flirted with other women, he never flirted with her either. Because after last night, perhaps that part, at least, would change.

She stared at the phone, willing him to call and end the suspense. She counted to one hundred, but it didn't ring. She counted backward from one hundred, but it still didn't ring. Disgusted with herself for literally waiting for the phone to ring, she picked herself up, changed to loose shorts and a T-shirt, then went for a power-walk. Hoping to fatigue her muscles enough to induce sleep, she tried to outstride her plaguing thoughts. Last night she had slept like the dead—the satisfied dead—but tonight looked doubt-ful.

The exercise provided enough solitude to rehash her sudden and seemingly persistent lapses in judg-ment—the infamous call, jeopardizing her job, lashing out at a lawman. Around and around her mind spun, dredging up more remorse on each pass. This was why she'd always been a good girl, had always fol-lowed the rules. Because she was no good at being naughty. At this age, the most debauchery she could successfully aspire to was exhibiting bad manners.

She returned an hour later, winded and perspiring, to find her apartment almost as warm as the outdoors, and her message light flashing. With fingers crossed ridiculously, she pushed the Play button.

"Thank you for buying this Temeteck product! This is a test message to allow you to adjust the volume. Press '1' if you don't want this message to play again."

She cursed and stabbed the "1" button, then stalked over to her blasted thermostat. "Eighty degrees?" she mumbled. "It's eighty degrees in my apartment." She turned the knob until sixty-eight appeared on the dis-play, but when she released it, the number flashed back to eighty, and there it remained.

Recognizing an impending breaking point, Georgia forced herself to take ten deep breaths of stale, hot air before she called the landlord. Even more irritated at not reaching a live person once she did call, she left an unladylike message about the broken thermostat.

Under the rush of a cool shower, she leaned into the wall and allowed the water to run over her neck and shoulders until she felt somewhat refreshed. More than anything, she needed food in her stomach and a good night's sleep. In the morning, she'd have a better perspective on today's unsettling events.

But when her eyes were still as big as silver dollars at two in the morning, Georgia remembered the old saying about a clear conscience being the softest pillow.

She rolled onto her side and stared at the cordless phone, working her mouth back and forth in thought. Suddenly, the answer came to her. She would call Rob and leave a message of apology on his machine for him to listen to when he arrived home. She'd been too forward, and she'd made them both uncomfortable. They could start over.

Georgia reached for the phone and pressed the speed dial button.

8

KEN'S BEDROOM was as hot as a boiler room on the sun. The apartment manager had promised his building was next on the list for cooling system repairs, but the entire city was under siege. He threw his legs over the side of the waterbed, then felt his way to the window and propped it open with a book in a futile attempt to catch a breeze.

He hadn't yet slept. His mind kept replaying the events of the past twenty-four hours, which still seemed too fantastic to believe. The only conclusion he'd reached was that his behavior on the phone the previous night had been abominable. The worst part was that he didn't regret it as much as he should, partly because the woman intrigued him, partly because the woman infuriated him.

Ken ran his hand down over his face. But Georgia Adams's crankiness did not exonerate him. He dropped back onto his waterbed—just as the phone rang.

He shot back up, his heart pounding, then relaxed with a laugh. He'd looked up Robert Trainer's listing and discovered their numbers were one digit off from each other's. What were the chances she'd dial it wrong again? Besides, she'd said that Robbie Boy was out of town. It was probably the station dispatcher and, hell, he wasn't sleeping, so why not go on duty a few hours early?

Ken yanked up the phone on the third ring. "Hello?"

"Oh. Hi, it's...me."

He instantly recognized her voice, and his body stirred.

"I didn't expect you to be home," she said quickly. "I was going to leave you a message."

Ken bobbed up and down on his mattress. He could tell her she had the wrong number and hang up. She'd never know it was him. He could do the right thing, right now. The words hovered at the back of his dry throat.

"Wh-when did you get back in town?" she asked.

Or he could do the *compelling* thing, right now.

Ken swallowed and held the phone away from his mouth. "Not long ago. I came back because...because I wasn't feeling well." He pushed down the rising guilt. He'd run a quick info sheet on Rob Trainer today, and uncovered the bare essentials of the man's life—employment, address, background check. Did Georgia know everything about her boyfriend? Her own history was squeaky-clean, including volunteer work with the Red Cross.

"Are your allergies bothering you again?" she asked.

"Um, I guess." He manufactured a cough.

"I thought your voice sounded a little strange," she said, "but I figured it was my new phone. If you're under the weather, though, I'm doubly sorry to wake you. This can wait until you're feeling better."

"No!" he practically shouted. "I mean, um, I was already awake and I'm glad you called."

"Actually, I called to apologize," she murmured.

He wet his chapped lips. "For what?"

"For...disturbing you last night."

He smiled into the phone. "Don't apologize. I...enjoyed it."

"You did?"

"I've been thinking about it all day."

"You have?"

Especially when we were together. "Yes."

"I...was afraid you'd think I was being too forward."

Her little laugh was the breeze he'd been waiting for all night long. Ken closed his eyes. Rob Trainer didn't deserve her. "Not at all. You were wonderful."

She sighed, a silky sound that made him bite back a groan. "I wish you were feeling better," she said, her voice wistful.

Ken sat up straighter, careful to keep the phone away from his mouth. "I feel well...enough."

"Well enough?" She laughed again, and his body hardened. "Well enough for an encore?"

He slid back against the pillows and exhaled. "Absolutely." A protest swam in the recesses of his mind, but desire chased it away. Desire for Georgia Adams. Because as wonderful as his fantasies had been the night before, now he knew what she looked like, how her skin glowed, the way her hands moved. "What are you wearing?"

"Nothing," she whispered. "It's too hot."

He groaned, imagining her lying in bed, arms

stretched overhead, her back arched. She reached for him, bringing him to full erection within seconds. "Georgia, my God, you're so beautiful. Come to me."

"I'm here," she said. "Kiss me...touch me."

"My hands...on your shoulders, arms, stomach."

"Mmmmmm...lower."

"Oh, you're killing me."

"That's it. There."

Her string of telltale moans tested his endurance. When he couldn't stand it any longer, he said, "Wrap your legs around my waist."

"Mmmmmm. Make love to me...now."

The quick sultry request nearly put him over the edge, but he held back, wanting to prolong their encounter. Her hair spilled all around, long and dark against her tangled sheets. Her breasts jutted, her thighs...welcoming. Oh, God help him. "Ahhhhhh," he breathed, easing inside her tight channel. "Oh, yes."

"Mmmm...all the way," she urged. "Yes, deeper... faster."

He obliged, gritting his teeth to match her rhythm without losing total control. "Georgia, I can't...last long. You're too much."

"Oh, I'm almost there...yes..." She gasped, then cried out, a desperately divine sound that drained his energy and his restraint. Ken yielded to her intensity, then matched it, their moans mingling into one song. His muscles bunched, then eased with diminishing spasms.

A comfortable silence stretched between them as

they slowly recovered. His eyelids drooped. Georgia's sighs were definitely the cure for his insomnia.

"Are you sleeping?"

He blinked awake. "No." Then he laughed. "Well, almost. That was...incredible."

Her laugh was musical, like a wind chime. "Want to meet for lunch tomorrow in your office building?"

He plummeted back to earth, remembering that she believed she'd just shared an incredible experience with her boyfriend. Her lyrical laughter was meant for Rob. "Um, I think I'll stay home and try to shake this cold."

"I thought you said it was allergies."

"Yes. No. I'm not sure." He coughed as if a lung were in jeopardy.

"You sound terrible. I'll come by tomorrow to check on you."

"No! I mean, I wouldn't want you to catch something. I'll be fine, really."

"Are you sure?"

He felt weak with relief. "I'm sure. Your calls are all the medicine I need. Besides, not seeing each other in person for a few days will make things more... interesting." Was that him talking, purposely perpetuating a fraud?

"But you're still planning to go to Stacey's wedding Saturday afternoon, aren't you?"

When in doubt, dig thyself deeper into a hole. "Well...sure."

"I'm going early to help the bridesmaids dress, so I'll meet you there."

"Okay." He made a mental note to check for a gas leak since he'd obviously lost a few brain cells.

"Meanwhile, I hope you're feeling better soon."

She had the voice of an angel. "I'm feeling better already."

"Good. I'll let you go," she said softly. "Call me when you're back on your feet?"

Ken hesitated. Being on the receiving end of her misdirected phone calls was one thing, but initiating contact and impersonating her boyfriend... "Why don't you call me instead...tomorrow night?"

"Okay," she agreed. "I'll be working the blood drive tomorrow evening at the municipal building, but I'll call you when I get home."

"Great," he said, his mind already leaping ahead.

He kept the phone to his ear until the dial tone sounded, then fumbled around in the dark to replace the handset. He limped to the bathroom and turned on the light, squinting under the harsh illumination. A ten-minute hot shower did little to erase her from his mind. He toweled off quickly, his body still thrumming from their encounter, his ears still ringing with the cries of her release.

Leaning on the sink, he stared at himself in the mirror and rubbed his darkened jaw. Women had called him handsome, even rugged, but all he ever saw in his reflection was a too-big guy whose opportunities had been based more on his brawn than his brain. And, from his conduct of late, he was definitely proving everyone right who believed a big guy couldn't be a mental heavyweight.

Remorse descended on his bare shoulders, bowing

them. What was he thinking? He wasn't, of course. He, the man of steel who had vowed never to let his libido get in the way of good sense, had succumbed to a soft voice with an erotic vocabulary.

His watch lay on the sink. Ken smiled wryly. Today was his birthday—thirty-seven. Did men have a biological clock? He laughed. He'd have to ask Klone, who spouted all that touchy-feely stuff when he wasn't playing practical jokes. He winced in the mirror, hoping his partner hadn't planned a birthday surprise. Good old Klone, always trying to set him up with a cousin or a niece of Louise's, although frankly, he hadn't met anyone who piqued his interest and his mind enough to make the rigors of romance worthwhile.

Until now. And as luck would have it, she had no clue how good they were together. In fact, she didn't even like him. And to make matters worse, he was helping to further the *other* guy's cause. A guy who, from Ken's cursory check, had a slightly blemished past.

A whine from his bedroom broke into his perplexing thoughts. He wrapped the towel around his waist and padded to the nook next to the dresser where he'd made a bed for Crash, the pooch he'd accidentally struck. "Can't sleep either, boy?" Poor little guy—he probably missed his owner and was confused about his immobility.

The battered dog gave a little bark in response, then lowered its head.

Ken stroked the spot between Crash's ears that he seemed to like. The ad he'd placed in the newspaper for a found dog wouldn't run for another week. "Until then we're stuck with each other," he murmured. "Hey, remember that lady doc who bandaged you up?"

The dog looked at him with shining eyes.

"Well, besides being gorgeous, she's really hot, but there's this other guy, see, and—" Ken stopped and laughed wryly. "And let's just say if she ever finds out what I've done, I'd be *lucky* to be in the doghouse."

Crash lifted his head and barked his apparent agreement.

9

"SO NOW when I walk in, Dr. Baxter says 'Here's Nurse Terri who's always very merry,'" Toni boasted of her one-sided romance with the head of obstetrics. "It's so cute."

Georgia lifted an eyebrow. "The man made up a ridiculous rhyme to go with a name that isn't even yours, and you call it progress?"

"Well, you're having phone sex with your boyfriend of ten months and you call *that* progress."

Touché. "Just do me a favor and tell the guy your name, okay?"

"But he'll be humiliated to find out he doesn't know who he's been talking to."

"What about you, the person he's calling by the wrong name?"

Toni sighed. "I just keep hoping he'll glance at my name tag." She focused on something behind Georgia. "Uh-oh, here comes Dr. Story. See ya."

Georgia frowned after her friend who scooted down the hall. Dr. Story, the attending E.R. physician for her shift, did not look pleased, his mouth pinched into a pucker and his glasses low on his nose. And he was making a beeline for her.

"Good morning, Dr. Story."

"Nurse Adams," he acknowledged without moving

his lips. "I've been told that you accepted and cared for an animal yesterday in the E.R., but that couldn't possibly be correct because by taking in an animal, you would be putting our entire program in jeopardy, risking jobs, not to mention risking the lives of patients who, in an emergency, would prefer that the nearest facility *not* be closed due to health violations brought on by one willful nurse who is supposed to be setting an example for the entire nursing staff."

If he'd stopped for a breath, she would've defended herself. By the time he finished his tirade, however, she simply apologized and promised that the episode would not happen again.

"If it does," he warned, the end of his nose moving, "you will be fired on the spot."

His eyes qualified his threat—no severance, no letter of recommendation and no farewell party. He turned on his heel and marched away with clicking strides. Georgia swallowed hard. Second chances in this industry were rare, and she wouldn't blow it. At the moment, she resented Officer Medlock intensely for getting her involved with the mongrel—and for popping into her head last night while she and Rob were having...fun.

The memory warmed her still. Maybe Rob *was* the man with whom she could explore her fantasies, all of them. She smiled as she prepared the meds for rounds. Imagine—a man who, much like herself, presented a stoic face to the world, when deep down, he, too, was probably looking for someone to unlock his passions.

How remarkable that they'd found each other. She

kept smiling and nodding to herself, trying to ignore the nagging image of Ken Medlock's face inches from hers after he'd wrapped his big arms around her and squeezed a hunk of bread from her throat. So the man was...obliging. Big deal. Yes, ma'am. No, ma'am. So he'd saved a dog's life and hers in the space of a few hours. Wasn't that the man's job, for heaven's sake? She saved lives every day in the E.R., so if Officer Ken thought she owed him something for that pedestrian procedure he'd performed in the mall, he had another think coming, assuming there was much thinking going on between the big man's ears. She set her jaw and forced his face from her mind.

Thank goodness the day passed with relative ease. Especially nice since she'd be volunteering at the blood drive until late in the evening. She'd be ready to relax with Rob on the phone by the time she arrived home. A wonderful by-product of their sensual sessions was the great sleep afterward, despite the suffocating temperature in her apartment.

Georgia left the hospital around three in the afternoon, emerging in heat so oppressive, she was instantly worried about the turnout for the blood drive. Most people wanted to give, but many looked for a reason to "wait until next time." The heat was keeping people indoors under air conditioners, which had overburdened the power plants to the point of brownouts all over the city. An increasing number of the E.R. patient ailments were heat-related.

She fanned herself with a small notebook she found in her purse, conceding that hormones also rose with the temperature. That might explain why a straight-laced New Englander like herself was behaving strangely, having phone sex with one man while fantasizing about another. If it weren't a felony, it was, at the very least, an extravagant sin.

She aimed for her normal seat on the end of the bus stop bench, but halted in her tracks at the sight of a flapping yellow flyer on the post of a nearby sign. *Lost dog. Mixed breed, male, long multicolored hair. Answers to the name Tralfaz.* Georgia made a face. Tralfaz? No wonder the poor dog ran away.

After writing down the number listed at the bottom of the flyer, she pursed her mouth when a thought came to her. The police station was only a block or so away from the municipal building. Maybe she would drop the number off with Officer Medlock on the way. He'd probably taken the dog to an animal shelter, but she could at least make an effort—but only for the rather cute dog's sake, she told herself during the cramped bus ride.

She had never been inside a police precinct before. Amazing how the mere presence of so many uniformed officers could make one feel so conspicuous, as if within these halls, one's transgressions were as apparent as a swallowed coin in an x-ray. (Her sister had warned her, but she had to try it anyway.)

Inside, the place was chaotic—she hadn't realized so much criminal activity was going on in this adopted city of hers. She waited in line for twenty-five minutes to talk to an imposed-upon middle-aged man with eyebrows so bushy she couldn't help but stare.

"May I help you?" he barked.

"I'm looking for Officer Ken Medlock."

He looked her up and down, then gave her the most curious smile. "Is this about a police matter?"

Georgia glanced down at her white uniform, a fitted skirt and tailored blouse—she'd wanted to look her best this morning for her expected dressing-down from Dr. Story. Her hair was pulled back into a tight, rolled bun. She'd forgotten to remove her stethoscope, but otherwise she failed to see the humor in her appearance. "No, my business is personal."

His remarkable eyebrows climbed. "Oh?" Then his eyes widened. "*Oh.* Just a moment." He picked up the phone and spoke into it, then hung up, grinning. "Right this way."

She followed the man through a maze of hallways and bullpens, but grew increasingly uncomfortable when she realized they were picking up a crowd of officers along the way. What the devil was going on?

"Ken," the man bellowed. "Happy Birthday, man!"

Ken Medlock turned, caught her eye, then unfolded himself slowly from his desk, his face a mask of surprise. Georgia swallowed in dismay—the man was just as attractive as she remembered, darn it. His hair looked as if he'd been running his hands through it. Lucky hands.

"Well?" The bushy-eyebrowed man gestured toward her. "Didn't you bring your own music?"

She squinted at the man. Was he senile?

"What's going on?" Ken asked the people circling around.

"Klone got you a stripper for your birthday!" the man shouted. The group broke into raucous applause and whoops of encouragement.

Georgia froze. A stripper? They thought she was a *stripper?* She glared at Ken, whose eyes bugged, although he clearly wasn't as bothered by the idea as she.

She crossed her arms and mouthed, "Do something."

"Time out, guys," he shouted, T-ing his hands. When everyone quieted, he said, "Miss Adams here is a registered nurse at County."

Shocked silence fell around them. The man who had greeted her mumbled an apology, then melted away with the rest of the shuffling group. Her skin tingled with embarrassment and she was certain her cheeks were scarlet. Were her encounters with this man destined to be awkward?

When they were alone by his desk, he wiped an amused smile from his face with his hand. "Hi."

She was considerably less amused. "Hello."

"Sorry about that, ma'am. The guys around here can get a little carried away. Do you want some coffee or something?"

Oh, that "ma'am" thing was killing her. She wet her lips. "No. I came to give you a phone number."

His grin curled halfway up his handsome face.

"Not mine," she said with a frown. Polite, presumptuous beast. "I saw a flyer advertising a lost dog that sounded like the one you hit."

"Accidentally," he added wryly.

"Whatever," she said, fishing in her purse to retrieve the scrap of paper she'd written on. "Here."

"Thanks."

He didn't look too grateful, though. "Did you take him to the animal shelter?"

"No, I took him home with me."

She blinked in surprise. "Oh. Well. How nice."

"Did I get you in trouble at the hospital?"

"Yes."

"I'm sorry about that, ma'am."

"No, you're not. I told you plainly I wasn't allowed to tend the dog, but you wouldn't leave."

"He might have died."

She shook her head. "Look, I like dogs as much as the next person, but how would you feel if you came into the E.R. with a heart attack and saw a dog lying in the bed next to yours?"

"That depends. Are you my nurse?"

"Goodbye, Officer Medlock."

"Wait. I was about to go on break. Want to grab a bite to eat?"

She did need to eat before going on duty for the blood bank, but she didn't want to eat with him. "No."

"Oh, come on," he cajoled. "No matter what you say, I saved your life yesterday. You owe me a hot dog or something. Besides, it's my birthday."

At the sight of his shining brown eyes, she wavered. He was impossibly appealing, that was certain. And although she could've saved herself yesterday, he *had* stepped in. "Well—"

"Ken," a man behind her yelled. "Happy Birthday, man!"

They were back, the entire crowd, escorting a blonde dressed in a traditional nurse's uniform. If nurses wore white miniskirts, that is. And five-inch heels. But the little cap that secured her bound hair was very convincing, and the black-rimmed glasses made the woman look almost smart enough to wade through the schoolwork necessary to become an R.N.

Georgia shrank back as the woman advanced and set a boom box on his desk, then pressed a button and began to undulate to a stylized version of "Happy Birthday" set to bump and grind music. Georgia's tongue settled into her cheek.

The woman tore off her nurse's cap, releasing her golden hair, swinging it in her customer's face. When the blonde began to unbutton her blouse, Georgia stumbled backward to the entrance, battling an onslaught of emotion. Some dark side of her wanted to see how the man would respond to the blatant display.

Officer Medlock was loving it. Not in a lecherous, lip-smacking kind of way, but in a good-natured, teasing kind of way. The woman was down to bikini top and skirt, wrapping her arms around Ken's neck as she danced around him. Georgia's eyes drooped as she imagined herself in the woman's place, peeling off her clothes for an audience of one.

But for whom?

Her eyes popped open. What was she thinking? When the woman pushed Ken into his chair and climbed onto his lap, she fled.

Georgia was glad to have a block to walk off her discomfiture before reporting for her volunteer work. Her steps were deliberately slow in the cloying heat, and she ducked under awnings whenever possible to escape the intense rays of the sun. But her breathing accelerated when she thought of the scene she'd just left. The *good* thing was that the performer's appearance had spared her Ken Medlock's company. Georgia worked her mouth from side to side.

The *bad* thing was that the performer's appearance had spared her Ken Medlock's company.

She shook herself, dismayed at her train of thought. At the sight of the blonde, he had instantly forgotten his invitation. Georgia pushed down the troubling images of sharing an intimate snack, then grabbed a jumbo pretzel from a street vendor, and hurried into the municipal building in anticipation of occupying her hands and her mind.

Since she'd given him the phone number of the likely owner of the dog, they had no further ties. In fact, Georgia could think of no circumstances whatsoever under which she and Officer Ken Medlock would be speaking in the future.

10

"I'D LIKE TO REQUEST Nurse Georgia Adams," Ken told the woman signing in volunteer donors.

She brazenly looked him up and down. "Are you a friend of Georgia's?"

No, but we've had sex. "She and I are acquainted."

The woman's face registered understanding. "Oh, wait. Are you the cop who nearly got her fired?"

He smiled wryly. "Well, I do have other claims to fame."

The woman eyed the nightstick at his side and lifted one thin eyebrow. "I just bet you do. Right this way, Officer Medlock."

He followed the skinny woman, amused that she appeared to know Georgia and Georgia's business. It occurred to him that the woman might be helpful. "Are you the friend of hers who's getting married?"

"Oh, no, that's Stacey Alexander. I'm Toni. Toni Wheeler."

He smiled. "Nice to meet you, Toni."

"Likewise," she said, fluttering her eyelashes.

He saw Georgia before she saw them. She was bandaging the arm of a middle-aged man who'd just finished giving blood. Her face was flushed with a smile as she pointed in the direction of a refreshments table. Ken experienced a stab of envy—he wanted to be the recipient of that radiant smile. Her profile was classically beautiful, and he asked himself for the umpteenth time why Robbie Boy hadn't slapped a ring on her dialing finger.

"Georgia," Toni said sweetly, "look who stopped by."

She turned her head and her smile dropped.

On the other hand, maybe her mood swings made Robbie Boy dizzy.

"Hi," he said, inclining his head.

"Hello."

Brrr. If the city could bottle that chill, the heat wave would be alleviated.

"Georgia," Toni said in a chiding voice, "you didn't tell me your cop was so cute."

"Is he? I hadn't noticed."

Toni gave Georgia a strange look, then handed her his sign-in sheet and scampered away.

"I'm not cute?" he asked, pulling his best hurt expression.

"What are you doing here?"

He swept his arm over the impromptu clinic. "I came to do my civic duty."

She lifted a sugary smile. "Are you sure your blood isn't too hot after your little birthday celebration?"

Apparently, she hadn't been amused. He squirmed, then grinned sheepishly, holding his hat in both hands. "I'm, uh, sorry about that. My partner gets a little carried away with practical jokes."

She seemed preoccupied with his form. "Hmm."

"Anyway, I tried to find you, um, afterward, but you'd disappeared."

She glanced up. "Look, Officer, I'm a little busy here. If you want to give blood, lie down."

He obeyed, thinking it might be his only chance to be close to her and prone at the same time. She put the blood pressure cuff on his arm, her mouth set in a straight line as she listened with her stethoscope.

He laughed. "From your expression, I must be dead."

"No, but your blood pressure is on the high side of normal. Is that typical?"

"No, it's always been perfect." But then again, his body was now trained to come alive at the sound of Georgia's voice. "Probably the excitement of the day. Can I still give?"

She nodded. "But have your blood pressure checked again in a few days just to be safe. Roll up your sleeve, please."

He unbuttoned the cuff of his blue uniform shirt. "We didn't get to have that hot dog. What time do you get off?" *Besides every time we talk on the phone.*

"Not for a few hours," she said, her expression one of total lack of interest.

The woman would take a scalpel to him if she knew he knew the sounds she made when she climaxed.

"And," she added, "you'll need to eat something as soon as you're finished here."

He didn't push, only because he had the promise of her call again tonight, assuming she hadn't yet figured out she was dialing the wrong number. Besides, the more time they spent together, the more likely she was to recognize his voice. Although, he realized their nightly phone rendezvous were numbered, since her boyfriend would surely call her soon and she'd realize her mistake.

She crossed her killer legs as she made check marks on his form. The woman was infinitely more titillating than that two-bit dancer the guys had hired.

Georgia leaned into him, sharing a whiff of her subtle fragrance, then tied a thick rubber band just above his elbow. She had a European look about her, with flawless skin, sleepy eyes and ultrafull lips. Exotic, in an understated way. Not the kind of woman who would stand out in a room, unless a man were extremely choosy. Her hair was rolled into a dark tight knot on her crown. He longed to see the silky length falling around her shoulders, like it would be tonight when she called.

Her fingers skimmed across his skin with the touch of a butterfly, and to his amazement, he began to grow hard. He slid his hat across his lap as inconspicuously as possible to cover the telltale evidence, but she saw the movement and frowned.

He averted his gaze and whistled tunelessly until he had himself back under control. The woman was addictive.

She turned over his arm and rather painfully flicked her finger against a network of veins at the bend. "There's a good one," she said, the hint of a smile on her mouth.

Of course, when she held up the needle she was going to stick into his arm, he knew why she was smiling.

"Careful, ma'am," he said. "I'm a sensitive— *owwww!*"

At last he was the recipient of that radiant smile. "That didn't hurt now, did it?"

He grimaced as she inserted the tube leading to a plasma bag into the end of the syringe. "Not much more than a hot poker in the eye."

"Since your blood pressure is up, you should bleed quickly," she said cheerfully.

"I suppose that's good?"

She smirked. "Unless you're run down by a police car."

He smirked back. "And brought to you for help?"

"I help any *person* who comes into the E.R.," she said, "even an impertinent, bossy person."

He wagged his eyebrows. "Oh, but I can be an animal sometimes."

"Just bleed, will you?"

But she seemed pleased that she'd gotten a rise out of him. The problem was, with all her fidgeting and adjusting, she was getting too much of a rise out of him. Her phone call tonight couldn't come soon enough.

"Did you find the dog's owner?" she asked.

Her voice sounded not quite friendly but...normal, at least. "I called, but Crash wasn't their dog."

"Crash?"

He shrugged his free shoulder. "Figured I'd better name the little fellow seeing as he might be staying at my place for a while."

She stroked the tube in a pulling motion, facilitating his blood being drawn into the bag. "Does that pose a problem spacewise?"

A few seconds passed before he realized she was actually conversing. "Um, no, my place is old, but pretty big. And it's just me living there."

"Oh."

So much for conversing. "Do you live alone?" he asked.

"That's absolutely none of your business."

He'd botched it again. "I meant do you live with your family?"

"No."

Not a chatty Cathy, this one. "Do you have a big family?"

"One sister, two nieces, all in Denver."

He remained silent in hopes she would elaborate.

"My father died several years ago, but I still have my mother. She lives with my sister most of the time."

She looked wistful and Ken thought of all the glad and sad moments in her life he would never have a chance to share, the laughter and tears he would never have a chance to witness. Georgia Adams made him feel proprietary—in a noble way, of course. Well, okay, maybe *all* of his intentions weren't so noble.

"How about you?" she asked.

Ken blinked, so lost in her stunning blue eyes that he'd forgotten what they'd been talking about. "How about me what?"

She sighed as if he were a half-wit. "Do you have a big family?"

"One brother, four sisters, ten nieces and nephews."

"Wow."

He took her monosyllabic response as an invitation to continue. "My folks are alive and well in Virginia.

We kids are scattered, but we try to get together at least once a year."

"That's nice." She checked the bag. "And you're done—in record time, too."

Great. Just when he wanted to spend time with the woman, he'd set a record for bleeding.

She removed the catheter with deft fingers, and gave him a gauze pad to press against the point of entry while she made notes on his form.

"Would you like to have dinner sometime?" he blurted.

At least he had succeeded in getting her attention. He held his breath, but she shook her head. "I can't. Rob and I are...exclusive."

But we're good together, he wanted to shout. *You've been sharing your fantasies with me.* "Did your boyfriend make it back to town?" He knew he was treading on dangerous territory, but he couldn't help himself.

"Yes. But I forgot to mention your name to him."

He squinted. Was she blushing? "Don't worry about it," he murmured, sitting up. He wanted to pull her close for a long kiss, Rob and the crowd be damned. Instead he rolled down his sleeve and fumbled with the button.

Then to his surprise, she stilled his hands. "Let me." He raised his eyebrows, but she simply nodded toward the registration desk. "The line is backing up."

Oh, well, regardless of her motivation, Georgia made buttoning his shirt cuff an erotic act, fingering open the tiny hole and inserting the little gold disc. Ken wiped a film of perspiration from his forehead just watching her nimble fingers and knowing where they'd been.

"There." She gave him a brief smile that stole moisture from his mouth. "Thanks for giving—the blood bank is dangerously low."

"Glad to help. I wish there was more I could do."

"Maybe you could encourage your buddies to come down."

Never one to miss an opportunity, he grinned. "How many pints do you need?"

Her teeth were white, even, glistening. "As many as you can get."

"If I can get one hundred donors down here, will you have dinner with me?"

She bit into her bottom lip. "No. But I'll buy you that hot dog."

His heart fluttered with possibility. "Deal." He pushed himself to his feet. "I hope you have enough blood bags."

Her smile shook him. "Looks like I'll be working late."

He hesitated. Did that mean she wouldn't be calling him tonight? "Did you have plans?"

Georgia shook her head. "I'm supposed to call Rob when I get home is all."

Ken's mouth quirked with smug satisfaction. "Well, when you talk to him tonight, tell him I think he's a lucky man." He put on his hat, then touched the brim. "Ma'am."

11

GEORGIA INJECTED a teasing note into her voice, lest Rob think she were interested in the man. "He said to tell you he thinks you're a lucky man."

His laugh was abbreviated. "I don't remember from the gym what this Medlock guy looks like. Should I be jealous?"

She pressed her ear closer to the phone. His head cold had fogged his voice until she could barely hear him. "Of course not. I m-mean, the man isn't repulsive, but he's just not my type."

"Oh?"

"Kind of big and bulky," she said quickly, floundering for words. "And pushy." And he called her "ma'am," as if she were...special.

"Pushy? Well, I guess that's how he was able to get so many policemen down there to give blood."

"I suppose," she said, leaning back on the pillows she'd stacked against her headboard. It *had* been quite a sight, all those blue uniforms standing in line. One hundred and six donors. Ken Medlock seemed determined to get that hot dog—and her attention. Trouble was, he had it. She considered telling Rob about the impromptu deal, but then thought better of it, lest he think she was actually looking forward to spending time with the man.

"Rob," she said quietly, unable to identify the emotions pulling at her. "I know we've been having...fun...on the phone lately, but I was wondering if tonight we could just talk." The way Ken Medlock had wanted to talk today, about family and things that were important. She'd held back with Ken because she hadn't wanted to become invested in a virtual stranger, but she did crave that kind of camaraderie with Rob.

"Talk," he mumbled. "Sure. What do you want to talk about?"

"I don't know," she admitted, casting about for a topic. "How about us?"

"What about...us?"

She smiled and burrowed deeper into the pillows. "Well, what first attracted you to me?"

"That's easy. You're beautiful, smart, beautiful."

A warm, tingly feeling bloomed in her stomach. "That's sweet, but I wasn't fishing for a compliment. What do you think makes us a good couple?"

"Isn't it enough that I'm crazy about you?"

Her grin widened, and she closed her eyes—the words she'd been hoping for, spoken with ringing sincerity. "Are you happy with the way things are going between us?"

"I...guess so. Yes. Yes, I am."

"Good. So am I." Remembering her earlier conversation with Ken, she said, "Tell me more about your family and where you're from."

"I'm from...Cincinnati."

Georgia laughed. "I know that. I mean, what was

your childhood like? I don't even know if you have brothers and sisters."

"Oh, well, you know...I'd rather hear about you."

"What about me?"

"Have you ever told me why you became a nurse?"

She smiled. "I don't think so."

"So tell me."

Georgia squirmed against the pillow at her back as memories flooded over her. Not all bad, not all good. "I guess I was always the family fixer. My father worked a lot." And then there were George Adams's occasional affairs, which she wasn't ready to share. "My sister and my mother were so much alike, they communicated through arguing."

"So you were the peacemaker and the healer."

"I suppose. I was also into photography. When I was seventeen, I came upon a car accident scene and pulled out my camera. But when I developed the pictures, I realized I'd used all my film to capture the paramedics and a nurse who had happened by. They were amazing...selfless."

"There were survivors?"

"Yes," she whispered, the memory keen. "Everyone survived. I decided that the next time I came upon an emergency, I wanted to be able to do more than take a picture. I wanted to make a difference in people's lives."

He was quiet for a few seconds, then said, "You got your wish."

She gave a little scoffing laugh. "If I don't get myself fired for taking care of dogs."

"It was that cop's fault, not yours."

She sighed. "Well, he *was* trying to do a nice thing—he just caught me at a really bad time and put me in an awkward situation. In hindsight, I shouldn't have reacted so...strongly."

"I'm sure he feels the same way. Don't lose sleep over it."

She wouldn't, although the memory of the man hiding his arousal with his hat might make for a bit of sheep-counting.

"Anything else interesting happen today?" he asked.

She liked this change in him. Rob was never much on small talk, but she rather enjoyed sharing the ordinary bits of the day. "Not much happened today. But I did receive a letter from my mother, yesterday."

"Oh?"

"Even living across the country, she has the uncanny ability to make me feel twelve years old."

"Mothers are good that way. Did she give you grief about still being single?"

"W-well, sort of."

"Just doing her job."

She sighed. "I suppose. Is your mother just as bad?"

"Er, aren't they all?"

"When will I get to meet your parents?"

He lapsed into a coughing spasm. "Georgia, I'm suddenly not feeling very well. I think my medicine is wearing off. Could we—" He coughed again, longer and harder. "Could we finish this discussion some other time?"

"Sure," she murmured, sorry for her ill-timing. Darn Ken Medlock for stirring things up inside her.

Feeling awkward, she squirmed against her pillows. "How about—"

"I have to run," he cut in. "Call me tomorrow night?"

"Okay." But he had already hung up. She replaced the phone, chastising herself for being so inconsiderate while he was under the weather. They would have plenty of time to talk on Saturday at the wedding. Georgia noticed the light on her message machine was flashing; someone had called while she was talking to Rob. She pushed the Play button.

"Thank you for buying this Temeteck product! This is a test message to allow you to adjust the volume. Press '1' if you don't want this message to play again."

Georgia groaned and pushed "1." She hated the stupid machine. Maybe something was wrong with it. Hoping a bowl of ice cream would help her go to sleep—in lieu of an orgasm—she walked to the kitchen in T-shirt and panties, stood in front of the open freezer door for a couple of minutes to cool off, then carried the snack to the living room and dropped onto the couch.

An upholstered brick. She had furnished what was supposed to be the most comfortable room in the house with a beige upholstered brick. What on earth did Rob see in this horrid couch? She spooned in the first mouthful of Cherry Garcia, then wondered idly what Rob saw in *her*. He'd said she was beautiful, but did he see the secret side of her that loved to try on hats and eat ice cream in her underwear?

A few days ago, she'd been on the verge of calling it quits with Rob, but now...now she'd discovered this surprisingly erotic and vulnerable side of him. She was anxious to see him on Saturday, to see if he acted differently, more relaxed. Hopefully the phone sex would open other doors of communication; it had so far. Perhaps they would discover they had more in common than their penchant for detail and love of foreign films.

The phone rang, and she reached for the extension. "Hello?"

"You've been holding out on me," Toni accused.

Georgia laughed. "What are you talking about?"

"I'm talking about that big hunky cop who delivered the entire Birmingham city police department to our door. He's gorgeous, and you were so witchy to him!"

"Ken Medlock almost got me fired," Georgia reminded her.

"But he tripled the blood bank reserves single-handedly in a matter of hours."

"He only pulled that stunt so I'd have to buy him a hot dog tomorrow afternoon."

"Oh, how romantic!"

"Toni, the man knows he gets on my nerves, and this is just another way to get on my nerves. I went along with it because it was for a good cause."

"I think he has the hots for you. All that 'yes, ma'am-ing'—Lordy, he's downright fattening."

"Stop it!" She didn't want to think about it. More.

"I'm serious—it's probably all that phone sex."

"Okay, you lost me."

"Vibes! You're giving off sex vibes, Georgia, and the cop is picking up on them. Sex begets sex."

"I thought that to beget is to *have* sex."

"You know what I mean."

"Well, I'm not interested."

"Why not?"

She swirled her spoon in her bowl and frowned. "Because I have Rob, and I think we're finally getting over the emotional plateau we've been on for so long. He's starting to open up."

"That's good...I guess."

"Of course it's good. Why wouldn't it be good?"

"I don't know...the expression on that cop's face. I've never seen Rob look at you that way."

"You mean with ridicule?"

Toni laughed. "If you ask me, I think this Medlock guy is getting you all worked up, and Rob is getting the payout."

Her spoon clanged against the bowl. "That's absurd. And I don't take love advice from a woman who lets a man call her by the wrong name just to spare his ego."

Toni sighed. "I'm going to tell Dr. Baxter tomorrow."

"Good."

"I'm going to tell him I changed my name legally from 'Terri' to 'Toni.'"

"You're hopeless."

"I'd better let you go so you'll be rested up for your date tomorrow with Officer Medlock."

She rolled her eyes. "It's not a date. It's vending food in a public park."

"Did you tell Rob about it?"

She hesitated. "No."

"I rest my case. Night-night."

Georgia frowned at the phone, then, pretending it was Ken Medlock, bounced it off a stiff cushion. Who was he to barge into her life just when things were starting to go so well with Rob?

12

ALL MORNING LONG, Ken's moods swung between elation that he'd be seeing Georgia this afternoon for his victory "meal," and self-loathing for carrying the ruse this far. He'd had to cut the conversation short last night because she was venturing into territory that was likely to land him in deep hooey.

Things were getting out of control, namely, his attraction to the woman. Hoping that blockhead Rob had skipped town for good and this mess would somehow resolve itself, he'd called the man's office and was told by a messaging service that Rob was likely to return to Birmingham sometime Sunday. It didn't explain, however, why the man hadn't at least called Georgia from wherever he'd gone. The ingrate.

Still, Rob's loss was his gain, at least until Sunday when the fertilizer would hit the fan. For the next couple of days, he would try to win over Georgia. Maybe with the double whammy of finding out Rob wasn't the man she'd been talking to, and with Ken's unflagging attention, she would break up with the guy.

Ken scratched his temple with the screwdriver he had used to install a box fan in the window of his bedroom. On the other hand, was that the way he wanted to win over Georgia—through embarrassment and by default?

Besides, what the heck would he do with her if he got her? A woman like Georgia probably bought potpourri by the truckload. And the most important thing to him right now was being the best cop he could be. Darn it, the woman barely tolerated him and she was already treading on his concentration. How bad would it be if he had unlimited access to her? Bad. Very bad.

Thankfully, Georgia would have no way of tying the phone calls to him even after she discovered she'd been dialing the wrong number. His phone machine featured a mechanical voice with a generic message. As a police officer, his number was unlisted and protected, so it wouldn't show up on caller ID screens or work with those newfangled call-back features.

He sighed. And, as a police officer, his conduct was supposed to be of a higher standard than mere civilians. His own loneliness was no excuse for deceiving an innocent woman, even if at first he had thought her to be not so innocent. Sometime, somehow this afternoon he would find a way to tell her the truth.

Georgia (big grin), want to hear something funny?

Georgia (shaking head), you're going to laugh when I tell you this.

Georgia (stepping out of striking distance), you're not going to believe this, but...

Who was he kidding? He'd be lucky if the woman didn't filet him. He hadn't broken any written laws, but it didn't take a mental giant to recognize he'd tread upon several unwritten laws.

Geez, Louise, what was he going to do now?

He could simply forget about her, he decided, seeing as how she wasn't keen on him anyway. *He's not my type.* If she called him again accidentally, he could just tell her she had the wrong number and hang up. End of story.

He ran his hand over his face, trying to erase the image of her smiling face, bantering with him last night at the blood drive, maintaining that stern facade. Was he the only man who knew how uninhibited she could be?

From his bed on the floor, Crash barked, reminding Ken that there were more pressing matters than his infatuation with Nurse Georgia Adams. Since he'd pulled an early morning shift for an ill fellow officer, Ken had the rest of the day off to anticipate and dread his afternoon meeting with Georgia. She clocked out at three, so they were scheduled to meet at Herrington Park around three-thirty. He glanced at the clock. An hour from now.

"How about some fresh air?" he asked the dog.

Crash barked twice.

Ken gave the screws on the fan box mount a few more turns, then repacked his toolbox. "Okay, give me a minute to figure out how I can make you mobile, and we'll go to the park. Maybe I can figure out a way to come clean once she gets there." He stopped and appraised the bandaged dog as an idea popped into his head. "And maybe she won't kill me if I look impossibly cute."

"OH, HOW CUTE," Georgia murmured despite herself when she saw Ken coming toward her on the sidewalk. Not *him*, although he did look surprisingly different and less intimidating in jeans and a navy T-shirt, but the bandaged dog he pulled behind him in the little red wagon. What did Ken say he had named him—Crash?

"Hi," Ken said as they strolled up. "I brought some company, hope you don't mind."

"Not at all," she said, stooping to stroke the dog's fur. "He's a handsome fellow, isn't he?"

"He takes after me," Ken said with a big grin.

She gave him a crooked smile, trying her best to resist his charm. Darn the big man, and his energy pulling at her. In her weakened state, after a night of tossing and turning and a hectic eight-hour shift, she was susceptible. Her immunity to him was lowered, and it scared her. Plus her friend Toni hadn't helped matters by teasing her all day about her "date."

"I was afraid you'd changed your mind," he said.

Georgia gave the dog one last scratch on the head before standing. "No. Last-minute emergency." Of course, she couldn't very well admit the emergency had been her appearance—her hair was flattened by a sterile cap she'd worn most of the day. Her makeup had worn off long ago, and she hadn't brought replacements with her, nor was she about to ask Toni for spares. She'd brought khaki shorts and sandals to change into, but the plain pink shirt she'd hoped to leave on had been compromised by a teenager with food poisoning. Desperate, she'd bought a yellow T-shirt in the gift shop that said Laughter is the best medicine. A nice sentiment, but hardly worth twenty-four dollars.

Ken rubbed his flat stomach, the muscles in his forearm bunching. "Just gave me more time to work up an appetite."

And she'd bet the man could eat. From her nutrition classes, she estimated his weight, then took into account his probable activity level, and came up with an astronomical amount of calories he needed every day to maintain his build. *One* hot dog? The man could probably eat a dozen.

But he settled for two, loaded with relish, and a plain one for Crash. Georgia ordered another one with relish for herself, but was still rifling for cash when she realized Ken had already paid the vendor for their food and colas. "It was supposed to be my treat," she protested.

"The treat's all mine," he assured her, gathering their food in his arms. "Will you pull Crash?"

Feeling a little foolish, she picked up the handle of the wagon and followed Ken to a picnic table under a sprawling hardwood tree.

"Is this okay?" he asked.

"Sure." Her pulse jerked stupidly—she had no reason to be nervous. It wasn't as if they were on a date or something.

"Are you a photographer too?" he asked, nodding to her camera bag.

She blushed. "Amateur. It's an old manual 35 mm, but it takes decent pictures. I've been wanting to get some shots of the park anyway." She didn't add that a photo shoot also made their little get-together seem like less of a date to her.

"Would you be willing to take one of Crash?" he

asked. "I took out an ad, but I might have a better chance of finding his owner if I had a picture."

She hesitated, only because it would perpetuate their interaction.

"I'd be glad to pay you," he added.

"Nonsense," she said quickly, feeling foolish. "I'd be glad to take a couple if it meant reuniting him with his owner."

His smile was dangerously pleasing. "Thank you, ma'am."

Oh, my. "Are you off duty today?" she asked, gesturing to his clothing.

He nodded, arranging their food so they could sit facing each other. The picnic table gleamed with a fresh coat of forest-green paint. "I pulled early morning duty."

She lowered herself to the cool seat, glad she'd taken the time to pull her hair up and off her neck with a clip. "You must be tired."

He shrugged, sending lots of muscle into motion. She peeled her gaze away as he sat down. "I'm not used to getting much sleep—I have problems with insomnia."

Georgia blinked. "So do I."

He handed her a hot dog on a little paper plate. "It's probably our jobs, weird hours, the stress. You're a nurse—what do you do for yours?"

Georgia choked on her first drink of soda. *I have phone sex with my boyfriend. While I'm thinking about you.* She gulped air. Last week she was a frustrated almost-virgin, this week she was a phone wench.

Ken cocked his head. "Do you have problems swallowing?"

Wiping her mouth with a napkin, she frowned. "Not usually."

"So what about the insomnia?"

She chewed slowly, carefully, then swallowed. "Try to relieve some of the stress in your life."

"I exercise, but it doesn't seem to help."

Georgia fidgeted with her straw. "What about... your personal relationships?"

He stopped chewing. "What about them?"

"Well, do you...have any?"

"If you're asking if I have a girlfriend, I don't."

She tucked the tidbit away in her subconscious, then shook her head. "I mean friends—co-workers, neighbors."

"I know a lot of people, but I'm not sure if I'd call all of them friends."

"Bingo," she said. "You told me you were close to your family and now they're not around. You're probably in need of emotional c-companionship."

He lifted one dark brow.

Squirming on her seat, she spotted the dog and seized the ungraceful way out. "Like Crash. Pets are known to lower blood pressure and to relieve stress."

"It is nice having someone else around the place."

"I've been thinking about buying a pet myself," she admitted. "For the company."

"You don't live with your boyfriend?"

How did the man know every button of hers to push? "No." She was alone, with a couch like a stone.

His brown eyes danced. "So you two aren't that serious?"

"We're not engaged, if that's what you mean." Although if their relationship was progressing as she hoped, perhaps her mother could be reigning over wedding plans sometime in the near future.

"Have you ever been married?" he asked.

"No. You?"

"*Absolutely not.*"

Okay. No ambiguity there. She was wasting the afternoon with a dead-end flirt when she should be consoling her ill boyfriend and exploring the new dimension of their relationship.

Sights and sounds and smells and touches descended all around Georgia, and suddenly she couldn't get out of there fast enough. The blue sky, the cool breeze, the children laughing in the playground—all of it a ploy, to make her think that she was in charmed company. She took another bite of the hot dog, thinking the faster she ate, the sooner she could escape.

"I see a lot of bad domestic situations in my line of work," he said. "I'm sure you do, too."

She nodded, gobbling her food.

"Makes you wonder how the people got together to begin with."

She nodded, washing down a large bite with a deep draw on her soda.

"I mean, of all the people in all of the world, how are you supposed to know when you meet *the* right person?"

She wet her lips. "You just...know, I guess."

"So Rob is the right person for you?"

His words lingered in the air between them. Her first instinct was to tell Ken Medlock that it was none of his ma'am-ing business. But he was so intent, his eyes serious yet alight with friendliness. As if he were...concerned. "I think so," she said, the intimacies she'd shared with Rob so fresh in her mind. If he weren't the right person, what did that make her? Guilt and grease didn't marry well in her stomach.

Ken gave a little laugh. "The story of my life—a day late and a dollar short." He took another bite of his hot dog, just as if they weren't discussing...

What *were* they discussing?

This man, this virtual stranger, threw her off balance, made her feel as if her thoughts and her beliefs were up for negotiation. Such a charming, compelling personality, as large as his muscled body. He reminded her of someone... Her memory ticked backward until... She froze when the match fell into place.

Her father. Good-looking, with a winsome smile. So easy to love, so easy to forgive his faults. Her bedroom had been next to her parents', so she'd overheard their late-night arguments over his infrequent, but hurtful, infidelities. Her mother would cry and be morose for days, but he would bring her gifts and eventually coax a smile from her by whispering sweet things in her ear and kissing her neck.

Georgia stood up. "I have to go."

He wiped his mouth with his napkin. "Already?"

"Yes. Th-thank you for rounding up your comrades last night. Many of them signed up to give regularly."

"That's good," he said. "But I was hoping that you and I might have longer to talk today."

She brushed crumbs from her lap and fed her last bite to Crash. "Sorry, I still have to shop for a wedding gift for tomorrow."

"What about the pictures?"

With hurried hands, she removed the camera and took a couple of shots of Crash from different angles. "I'll mail them to you," she said as she crammed the camera back into the bag.

"I thought you were going to take some photos of the park."

"I changed my mind. Thanks for the hot dog."

"How about dinner?" he asked, standing. "Georgia, I'd like to get to know you better."

Her breath caught in her chest. Ken Medlock was too overwhelming, too...potent. She and Rob were intellectual equals, who now shared a sensual bond as well. She wasn't about to throw all of that away because she was physically attracted to a cocky self-proclaimed bachelor cop.

"I can't," she murmured. "Like I said, I have Rob."

He pursed his mouth.

She swallowed, and her ears popped with the released pressure.

"Did you tell him what I asked you to last night— that I think he's a lucky man?"

Georgia nodded.

"And what did he say?"

She inhaled. "He asked me if he should be jealous."

"And what did you tell him?"

"I told him no, because..."

"Because?"

Best to nip this flirtation in the bud. She exhaled. "Because you're not my type."

He crossed his arms over his chest, a small smile on his lips. "What type am I?"

She chewed on the inside of her cheek.

He leaned forward on the table, his face inches from hers. "Georgia," he said softly, "what type am I?"

Her throat convulsed. The type of man who could set her world on end. Send her spiraling into decadence. His eyes searched hers, and she was afraid of what he saw. She wanted to pull away, but their mouths were like inverse magnets, the attraction growing stronger exponentially as the space between them closed millimeter by millimeter.

Georgia didn't know what she expected, but the electricity of his lips meeting hers was an intoxicating, luxurious feeling of pure indulgence. Like eating white-chocolate-covered cherries while relaxing in a deep, fragrant bath as hot as the body could stand. She opened her mouth to receive him, flicking the tip of her tongue against his teeth in invitation. He accepted with a deep moan that vibrated inside her mouth, sending a stab of desire straight to her belly, and moisture to her—

Georgia pulled back, and covered her mouth with the back of her hand. What had she done?

He remained leaning forward, his mouth open a fraction, his brow furrowed. "Georgia?"

This was sheer lunacy. The man was a player, and she'd fallen for it. Mortified, she stumbled backward, away from the confining picnic table. "You're the type of man...who would kiss a woman who's involved with another man." She wiped at her mouth, breathing hard. "I...I don't like the way you make me feel. I try to be an honest person, Ken, just as I expect the man I'm seeing to be honest with me."

He didn't answer, just stared at her.

"You probably think that's old-fashioned," she said with an awkward but sober laugh. "But trust is very important to me."

A flush darkened his face. Perhaps she'd spoken too vehemently, but the words needed to be said, if only for her own ears. After all, if she were seeing Ken Medlock—not that she would—but if she *were* seeing him, she wouldn't be slinking around kissing some other man in the park.

"Goodbye," she murmured, then grabbed her purse and camera bag and practically ran to the bus stop two blocks away. Cool relief flooded her—she'd managed to disentangle herself from the man without totally dishonoring her relationship with Rob. Close call.

Rob. Remorse sat in her belly. Poor man, he was probably feeling neglected, down with a cold and her playing twenty questions on the phone last night. She'd been so inconsiderate—and she a nurse, for goodness sake.

When a thought struck her, she chastised herself for not thinking of it before—instead of a clandestine meeting with Ken Medlock, she should be fostering her romance with Rob. She'd stop at Claxton's Deli, pick up a big bowl of their chicken soup and drop by Rob's house.

Georgia turned toward her destination, a decided spring in her step. Rob would be so surprised.

The Harlequin Reader Service® —Here's how it works:

Accepting your 2 free books and gift places you under no obligation to buy anything. You may keep the books and gift and return the shipping statement marked "cancel." If you do not cancel, about a month later we'll send you 4 additional novels and bill you just $3.34 each in the U.S., or $3.80 each in Canada, plus 25¢ delivery per book and applicable taxes if any.* That's the complete price and — compared to cover prices of $3.99 each in the U.S. and $4.50 each in Canada — it's quite a bargain! You may cancel at any time, but if you choose to continue, every month we'll send you 4 more books, which you may either purchase at the discount price or return to us and cancel your subscription.

*Terms and prices subject to change without notice. Sales tax applicable in N.Y. Canadian residents will be charged applicable provincial taxes and GST.

If offer card is missing write to: Harlequin Reader Service, 3010 Walden Ave., P.O. Box 1867, Buffalo, NY 14240-1867

BUSINESS REPLY MAIL
FIRST-CLASS MAIL   PERMIT NO. 717   BUFFALO, NY

POSTAGE WILL BE PAID BY ADDRESSEE

HARLEQUIN READER SERVICE
3010 WALDEN AVE
PO BOX 1867
BUFFALO NY 14240-9952

NO POSTAGE
NECESSARY
IF MAILED
IN THE
UNITED STATES

13

ROB'S HOUSE WAS a forty-minute walk from the nearest bus stop, but Georgia didn't mind. The weather was wonderful, if hot, and she had plenty of thinking to do. Ken Medlock's interest in her was flattering, but fleeting, she was sure. She knew Ken's M.O.—the man saw her simply as a challenge, a conquest. Rob, on the other hand, had taken her out regularly for many months now. And they were finally progressing toward the kind of physical relationship she desired. She would be crazy to mess it up now.

Her first thought when she saw Rob's beautiful two-story gray brick home was that she'd never seen his lawn so unkempt. Her second thought was that it must be driving him crazy, lying in bed with a cold while his Bermuda grass went to seed. But at the sight of the newspapers stacked on the stoop, alarm blipped through her. The fact that Rob hadn't been able to retrieve his beloved *Wall Street Journal* meant that he was more ill than he had allowed her to think.

She stepped over the stack of papers, then balanced her purse and the canister of soup to ring the doorbell. After a couple of minutes with no response, she rang it again, perplexed. With no answer, she dug the copy of the door key he'd given her from her wallet and carefully unlocked the front door.

"Rob?" she called in the direction of the upstairs. She walked into the foyer, frowning at the dim lighting. "Rob?"

Concerned now, she set down her purse and the soup, then jogged up the staircase and to the right of the landing into the master suite. Not only was he not in his bed, but the massive four-poster king looked like it hadn't been slept in recently. Rob was nothing if not neat. She'd only been in the suite a handful of times, usually when Rob wanted to show her a new book in his collection of first editions or to retrieve a Band-Aid from the bathroom vanity, but everything appeared to be in place—not even signs of sickness, like medications or boxes of tissues. As always, his surroundings were impeccable.

She checked the other upstairs bedrooms, then descended to the first floor, once again calling his name. Moving quickly from room to room, she scoured the first level, then walked down into the daylight basement, which had been turned into a gaming area and bar, and finally opened the door from the mud room leading to the garage.

A little laugh escaped her. Why hadn't she checked here first? His black Lexus was missing—he'd probably gone to the office, or maybe even driven himself to the drugstore. Relieved, but disappointed to have missed him, she found a pen and a piece of paper to leave a note.

Rob,
I came by to cheer you up with chicken soup and TLC. Sorry I missed you—hope this means you're

feeling better. Left soup in the refrigerator.

Georgia chewed on her lip, conjuring up the nerve to write something more provocative. She inhaled deeply. After what they'd shared together, she could be brave.

Call me tonight if you feel like having a little X-rated fun on the phone. ☺ See you at the wedding tomorrow.

Georgia.

She propped up the note on the black granite counter against a state-of-the-art combination coffee grinder and brewer, moved the newspapers to a table inside the foyer, then locked the door behind her. On the way back to the bus stop, she rubbed the area just beneath her breastbone—that spicy hot dog wouldn't allow her to forget about the little tête-à-tête with Ken Medlock. Everything about the man was an inconvenience.

His face continued to haunt her as she shopped for a wedding gift from Stacey's twenty-seven-page registry at a housewares specialty shop. But she attributed the pesky vision to his wholly improper line of questioning this afternoon.

"Have you ever been married?"

"No, you?"

"Absolutely not."

After hearing a response like that, any sane woman would avoid Ken Medlock at all costs. Why even entertain the thought of being attracted to a man who was cocky enough to issue a warning up front about his commitment capacity?

From the endless selection of delicate china patterns, ringing crystal and mirror-shiny silver services, she chose a large pewter platter with a raised grapevine pattern. She'd read somewhere that people always gave the gifts they wanted for themselves, which was true in this case, she admitted. To her, platters connoted family gatherings and memories made, a blessing she wanted for her friend Stacey...and someday, for herself.

In her mind she pictured a Thanksgiving table featuring a perfectly browned turkey, a dazzling array of impossibly delicious side dishes, and dozens of sweatered arms reaching for more than their share. In-laws, friends...children.

She panned the smiling faces, basking in the warmth of their love. Then she stopped and frowned. What the devil was Ken Medlock doing sitting at the head of her table?

He winked and lifted his hand in a little wave. Presumptuous sod.

She bought the platter and jockeyed it home via the bus, walking into her sauna of an apartment around seven o'clock. She deposited her bags in the living room with a sigh, then smiled at the flashing light on her message machine. Rob had probably called to thank her for the soup. She pressed the Play button.

"Thank you for buying this Temeteck product! This is a test message to allow you to adjust the volume. Press '1' if you don't want this message to play again."

Georgia pressed the "1" button five, ten, twenty

times, each time faster and harder than the last. She broke a nail, and her promise to stop cursing aloud. The owner's manual yielded nothing other than a headache and a dent in the wall when she threw it. First thing tomorrow, the blankety-blank phone system was going back to the place where she'd bought it.

She was still grumbling under her breath when the object of her consternation rang. Hoping it was her super telling her the month's rent would be waived due to the unbearable conditions, she snatched it up.

"Hello?"

"Georgia, dear, must you always answer the phone as if you just finished running a marathon?"

Georgia sat on the coffee table, which, she noticed, was more comfortable than the couch. "Nice to hear your voice, too, Mom. Are you having a good time with Fannie?"

"Of course. Her home is *so* luxurious, I feel as if I'm on vacation."

"That's nice. How are the girls?"

"Precious."

"And Fannie?"

"Missing Albert—he's traveling for business. They adore each other, you know."

"Yes, Mom, I know."

"Did you get my letter?"

"Yes, thank you for lighting a candle for me."

"A mother's job."

She frowned. Weren't those Ken's words?

"I saw on the news that Birmingham is under a dangerous heat wave, and I wanted to see if you were okay."

"It's hot, and my air conditioner isn't working, but I'm surviving."

"Good. Do you and Bob have big plans for the weekend?"

"It's *Rob*, Mom, and as a matter of fact, we're going to a wedding."

She clucked. "Are you getting serious about this young man?"

Georgia reached for a cord to fidget with, then remembered the phone was cordless. "I...don't know. He's...nice." And safe. She frowned. Where had that thought come from?

"Nice? He has his own business and a home—you'd better snap him up."

Her mother saw the world in such simple terms. "But I'm not sure I'm in love with Rob."

"Love?" Her mother made a tsk-tsking sound—she had an entire repertoire of chiding noises. "You're not getting any younger, Georgia."

"Mom, I'm only thirty."

"By the time I was your age, I'd been married for thirteen years."

Georgia bit her tongue to keep from uttering something regrettable—her mother couldn't help that she'd fallen for a smooth-talking philanderer. "Mom, I still have lots of time to settle dow—"

"Oh, there's Fannie, I have to go, dear. Tell Bob I said hello."

She sighed. "Okay, I'll tell him."

"Toodleoo, dear."

"Toodleoo." She disconnected the call, shaking her head. No doubt her poor mother had endured a rocky marriage, although she'd never discussed it with the girls. It was obvious that she was living vicariously through her daughters, mainly Fannie, but Georgia knew she truly wanted them both to be happy.

But she sorely missed her father.

Georgia gave the thermostat a swat as she walked toward the shower, peeling off her clothes. Her earlier thought sprang to mind. Rob was *safe*? Safe wasn't a characteristic, safe was a, a, a...place.

Had she been so affected by her father's indiscretions that she had projected love on to a man who was as opposite from George Adams as was earthly possible?

She stepped under the cool spray and tilted her head back until her hair was saturated and heavy. She sighed as the day's stress began to wash away.

And conversely, had she shunned the interest of the man who reminded her very much of her irresistible father? Ken Medlock's dancing brown eyes mocked her, challenged her.

You did a bad, bad thing, Georgia. You know you want me. I can take you places you've only dreamed of going. Unsafe places.

"I went there with Rob," she murmured.

But you were thinking of me. I was in your mind before you even met me.

She slid the loofah glove over her hand, reveling in the nubby texture and the bulk, the glove resembling a man's hand...a lover's hand...Ken's hand. She resisted the pull of him, his smile, his big body, seemingly built to plague her. Georgia ignored the alarms going off in her head. Perhaps a little fantasy would help get him out of her system. He owed her that much...

Georgia leaned over and began sudsing her feet with the loofah in little therapeutic circles. The water, the rhythmic movement, the aromatic soap. Inch by inch, she rubbed the cleanser into her ankles, calves, thighs, wondering if Ken had a slow hand, or would rush to pleasure her.

Whichever you like, Georgia. I'm at your bidding, ma'am.

He was so earthy, definitely a man in tune with his body. The sheer size of him sent a thrill through her. His mouth... He was a wonderful kisser, strong, firm, insistent. She lifted her head and allowed the water to pulse over her mouth and spill off her chin. She resumed her massage, methodically moving over her thighs, to her buttocks, to her stomach, moving in circles around her navel, triggering a slow grind of her hips.

Happy Birthday, Ken.

She closed her eyes and imagined putting on a show for him alone. He stood outside the shower in his uniform, barred from entry, able only to watch through the fogged glass.

With the loofah, she touched her breasts, outlining their contours, working inward in slow, firm circles.

Do you like?

He could only nod, which made her smile, smug with feminine power. Such a big, strong man. So malleable in her hands.

She moved the glove over her nipples and moaned, rubbing until they glowed bright pink beneath the white suds. Then she removed the hand-held shower head, turned the water to pulsate, and rinsed the soap from her body, moving slowly from neck to waist, lingering at her thighs before she leaned over seductively to give him a shocking angle while she finished her calves and ankles.

Come out here. I want to touch you.

She turned off the shower and stepped out of the glass stall to towel off slowly and prolong his torture. But when she looked up, he was gone.

The rush of disappointment was keen, overridden quickly by sobriety. She laughed, a hollow little sound in the confines of the tiled room. Of course he was gone. It was her subconscious speaking to her—men like Ken Medlock didn't stick around for long.

But her body still shook from the stimulation, and her breasts fairly ached. She stumbled to the bedroom, longing leadening her limbs. She felt...engorged, ready to come out of her skin.

The light from the bathroom cast just enough illumination for her to find her way to the bed. She fell across the comforter and hugged herself, squeezing her eyes shut against the fantasies that played behind her eyes. Ken Medlock was in her fantasies only because she had seen him so many times over the past couple of days. His face and body were fresh in her mind. She just needed to see Rob, that's all. To be reminded of his blond good looks, his lanky build, his well-shaped hands. She rolled over and stared at the phone in the dark.

Maybe he had called her and wasn't able to leave a message on that fouled-up machine of hers.

Her womb clenched with pent-up desire. It was either call, or fly solo with Ken Medlock's kiss in her head.

She reached for the phone.

was to try to help. I had to do something to cool things.

He groaned, jammed the pillow over his head, then—

Screw it. He kicked off the sheet and fought his sheet and stood.

14

ALTHOUGH THE BOX FAN had cooled his room some-what, Ken lay wide awake, his body fatigued but his mind on a treadmill. It had taken all his effort not to go after Georgia today. Never before had a kiss shaken him so. He was falling for the woman, like a big stupid tree. He sighed and pulled a hand down over his face. There was no good ending to this scenario, at least not for him.

When the phone rang, he turned his head on the pil-low, stopping short of a prayer. He couldn't very well ask to be led unto temptation, could he? He reached out in the darkness and picked up the phone on the third ring, covering the mouthpiece with a handker-chief, just in case. "Hello?" He held his breath in the silence. One...two...three. "Hello?" he repeated.

"Hi. It's Georgia."

His breath whooshed out in relief. "I'm glad."

She made a happy little noise that clutched at his stomach. "Did you try to call?"

"I...was getting ready to," he said cautiously, wish-ing he had the nerve to come clean. The woman had already turned him down for a date. What did he have to lose?

Her stolen kisses. Her respect. Her calls.

"I just got out of the shower," she whispered. "It

was so hot in here, I had to do something to cool down."

He groaned. Just one last ride, he promised himself. She was so unbelievably sexy, and the fun would end Sunday night when her boyfriend returned, if not sooner.

"Problem is," she said, "I'm still hot."

His erection tented his pale-blue boxers. "It's getting warmer in here by the minute. What are you wearing?"

"A towel."

Lucky, lucky towel.

"What about you?" she asked.

He heard seams splitting as he shed his boxers. "Nothing. God, I haven't been able to get you off my mind."

She murmured her pleasure. "I was wondering... How do you feel about...oral sex?"

He swallowed. "I'm in f-favor of it."

She laughed.

Ken lay back against the pillows and closed his eyes as she uttered erotic words. She knelt over him and took his throbbing rod into that wonderful mouth of hers, flicking her tongue like when he'd kissed her today. Her dark hair fell forward like a feathery curtain, tickling his abdomen. When the ministrations brought him close to the brink however, he instructed her to swing her body around so he could return the favor. He moaned against her musky sex, tonguing the center of her control until she lost it, grandly. His climax followed soon after, quick and intense.

"That was wonderful," he breathed. "I can't imagine anything you would do that I wouldn't love."

She laughed. "I thought the word 'love' wasn't in your vocabulary," she said, her voice breathless and teasing.

Hmm. Rob had never told Georgia that he loved her? "I, um, changed my mind. The last few days..." What? These last few days he'd fallen for her while impersonating her boyfriend?

"Go on," she urged.

He squirmed, not wanting to put words in the man's mouth. "I just feel different about us."

She sighed. "And I was so afraid you wouldn't like this."

"Are you kidding? I can't wait to see you again." That had just slipped out. Ken winced and waited.

"You gave me a scare today," she said.

Ken frowned. "When?"

"When I dropped by your house," she said with a little laugh.

His heart skipped one beat, two beats.

"When I saw the papers stacked up on the stoop, I was worried that you were more ill than you told me. I could just picture you upstairs, withering away in that humongous bed of yours."

Speaking of withering.

"I finally looked in the garage and saw your car was missing. Did you go in to the office?"

His mind raced, trying to keep up with the lies and the half truths. "Um, yes."

"I figured your cold had put you behind," she said. "You sound much better, by the way."

"I'm still a little hoarse," he insisted, then cleared his throat for effect.

"I suppose you got my note." She laughed, then paused expectantly.

He nearly dropped the phone. "I, uh...I—no."

"I left it on the kitchen counter."

"Ah." He cast around for an explanation. "It was dark when I got home and I didn't even turn on a light."

"Oh, well," she said. "I just wanted to let you know I left you soup in the refrigerator."

Ken frowned. "That was nice of you."

"Happy to do it. And I'm glad to hear you're feeling better. I guess this means you'll be at the wedding tomorrow."

He froze. Would Rob be back in time to attend the wedding? "I'm...planning to. If I don't get caught up...at the office."

"Oh," she said, clearly disappointed.

Did Rob disappoint her often?

"Remind me again where the church is," he said in his best guys-will-be-guys voice.

"St. Michael's, silly. Remember, you pulled some strings and got them a deal on printing their invitations?"

"Of course." Ken winced. "Except I don't recall the time."

She sighed. "Three-thirty."

"Right," he said. "Three thirty." Far away, a siren screamed, barely audible over the whir of the fan, but his ears were attuned to the noise of emergency.

Crash scratched against the floor, obviously trying

to stand. He barked, several times, ending in a whine—he'd heard the siren, too. Like an idiot, Ken waved his arms to quiet the dog, then bounded into the bathroom and closed the door.

"What was all that noise?" she asked.

"The television," he said, sitting on the edge of the tub. "Some cop show."

"Oh," she said flatly.

"How's work?" he asked, partly to change the subject, and partly because he wanted to know.

"Dr. Story is watching me, waiting for me to make another mistake. He called me in this morning to sign a report he wrote up about that incident with that policeman I told you about."

Ken swallowed guiltily. "Oh?"

"That little stunt he pulled will go on my permanent file."

He was torn between commiserating with her and taking up for himself. "Well, I guess knowing you did the right thing will have to be its own reward."

"Hey, whose side are you on, anyway?" She laughed, and he found himself irritated that she seemed so damnably cheerful around her boyfriend all the time. She yawned, then her laugh tinkled over the line again. "I'm sorry—I'm suddenly so sleepy."

Ken frowned. He wished he could say the same, but he had enough on his mind to keep a dozen men tossing and turning. He didn't want to let her go, but he couldn't very well keep her on the line. "I guess I'd better say good-night, then."

"That's funny."

He picked up on an odd note in her voice. "What?"

"You sound so...different."

He adjusted the handkerchief and moved farther away from the mouthpiece. "It's just my cold."

"No," she said, sounding troubled. "I don't mean your voice. I mean...never mind."

"Georgia," he said, overcome with frustration. "I love...talking to you."

She was silent for so long Ken was afraid she had fallen asleep. At last she murmured, "Good night, Rob," and hung up.

GEORGIA HADN'T FELT so thoroughly miserable in recent memory. Her body still pulsed from a release she'd shared with Rob...while she fantasized about another man. And the mind could play devious tricks on a person—she'd even begun to imagine Ken Medlock's voice in Rob's scratchy one.

Was this roiling sensation in her stomach what her father felt when he came home to kiss her mother's neck after a bout of fooling around? Could she even face Rob tomorrow if he showed up for the wedding?

She squeezed a handful of pillow into her fist. Rob didn't deserve this, this...distraction. Not when things were going so well between them. He'd never been so carefree, so vulnerable. For months she'd been hoping for a sign that he was open to exploring a deeper, more intimate relationship. Yet tonight when she'd thought he was going to tell her he loved her, she'd panicked.

"What does that mean?" she whispered aloud in the dark.

It means you're like your father. Never appreciating what

you have, always wanting what is out of reach, or things you know are bad. Or wrong. Or hurtful. Willing to sacrifice warm security for hot passion. Self-indulgent. Reckless. Wicked.

Georgia sighed and flung the sheet off her humid body. *And hot.*

15

"WHAT DOES IT MEAN?" Toni repeated over the phone. "I'll tell you what it means—you are falling for the cop."

"No, no, no," Georgia said, shaking her head. "Wrong answer." She sat down on her coffee table and put her feet up on her couch. "Just because I have a couple of harmless little fantasies about the guy doesn't mean I'm falling for him."

"If they were so harmless, then why are you making such a fuss?"

Good question.

"And what about the kiss?"

She was beginning to regret telling her friend everything. "The kiss happened in the heat of the moment—completely unplanned. It meant nothing."

"If it meant nothing, then why are you in such an uproar?"

"Because I feel guilty!"

"If you've done nothing to be ashamed of, you shouldn't feel guilty."

"You aren't Catholic. And I have this fear that Rob will run into Ken in the gym, and Ken will casually mention that we kissed in the park."

"So when you see Rob at the wedding today, tell

him about it and let him know it didn't mean anything."

Georgia blinked back sudden tears and made choking sounds.

"It did mean something, though, didn't it?"

She dropped her forehead into her hand. "Maybe," she whispered, sniffing.

"Georgia," Toni said, her voice incredulous. "Meeting someone who makes you feel extraordinary is something to *celebrate*, not cry over."

"But what about Rob? Things were just starting to go so well."

"I think your interest in the cop simply means you're not ready to settle down right now. It's not a crime, and Rob might be hurt, but he'll live."

Georgia lifted her chin. "You're absolutely right."

"So what are you going to do?"

"I have no idea."

"I DON'T KNOW what's wrong with it," Georgia told the clerk, then scooted a box full of the phone, message recorder and wires across the counter. "But the only message I've gotten in a week was the mechanical one about adjusting the volume."

The kid scratched his head and gave her a sullen expression. "You're returning this phone system because no one ever calls you?"

She smiled sweetly—he was the obviously the author of the manual. "*No.* I'm returning this phone system because a friend of mine told me she has left at least two messages I never received."

"Got your receipt, lady?"

She slid it across the counter.

His hand disappeared below the counter to scratch someplace she couldn't see. "One of our repair guys will have to take a look at it tomorrow. Can we call you?"

She leaned forward, pushed back the straw hat she had bought for today, and enunciated very clearly. "That would be fine, except now I don't *have* a phone. How about you tell me what time tomorrow I can come back."

They negotiated a time, and Georgia exited the store, aware she was garnering a few strange looks because not everyone in the electronics store wore a long sheer dress, a straw hat, and white wedge espadrilles, plus carried a huge wrapped package with a big silver bow.

She caught a bus at the corner of the shopping center, then walked a half block to the church, replaying her conversation with Toni. She was right, of course. If Georgia was so distracted by Ken Medlock, she wasn't making herself wholly available to Rob. It was the pushing and pulling that was making her crazy. The prudent thing to do was to suggest to Rob that they take a break from seeing each other.

She entered the church from the back and followed the sound of raised voices and female laughter down a hallway to the room where the bride and bridesmaids were dressing for their photos. She had never seen so much clutter—clothes, shoes, makeup bags, hair appliances. Stacey looked ethereal in ivory. Her mother fussed with her train while another older woman worked on the bride's chin-length red hair. Toni was one of four bridesmaids dressed in long, straight-skirted gowns in a deep coral color.

"You look beautiful," Georgia said.

Her friend blushed prettily and handed Georgia a curling iron. "Will you curl the back of my hair?"

She helped to arrange Toni in front of a mirror and set to work.

"I don't suppose Rob is here yet?"

Georgia shook her head. "He said he might get hung up at the office since he's so behind from being sick." She couldn't decide whether she wanted to get the breakup over with, or put if off another day.

"You'll look back on this someday and laugh," her friend offered.

"Think so?"

"Yeah, when you and the cop have six kids."

Georgia laughed good-naturedly. What she hadn't told Toni was that while she *was* planning to break off with Rob, she *wasn't* planning to go out with Ken Medlock.

"Too bad you couldn't have broken up with Rob before and asked that yummy uniform to bring you to the wedding."

She gave a noncommittal nod. She was taking a hiatus from men—dating them, even merely *looking* at them, had awakened her dark side. She needed time and space to regain her perspective.

Toni kept glancing in Stacey's direction with a wistful expression. "Think you or I will ever be brides, Georgia?"

An amusing question, since Toni was two years

younger. "Probably. Someday. How goes it with Dr. Baxter?"

Toni made a face. "I haven't told him my name yet."

"Toni!"

"I can't help it. He calls me Terri Strawberry now. How cute is that?"

"How *sexist* is that?"

"I know, I know. I'm going to tell him, no matter how embarrassing it is."

"Good."

Georgia finished curling her hair, sliding her own envious glances toward the glowing Stacey—not because the woman was getting married, but because she was marrying someone she was head over heels for. And Neil seemed to be head over heels for her, too. Georgia looked around the room, surveying the happy, fretting women, taking in the buzz of conversation and hair dryers, acknowledging the charge in the air. Excitement. Happiness. Optimism.

She wanted it. She wanted true love and all the trappings of giddiness. And someday she'd have it...if these overactive hormones of hers didn't get in the way.

Georgia smiled and nodded at another bridesmaid who needed an extra hand with her hair. She dreaded the talk with Rob, but she was grateful for one thing— she'd left Ken Medlock yesterday in the park with a stern rejection, and if she mailed the pictures of his dog, she couldn't imagine a reason why she'd ever run into him again.

KEN WALKED PAST the job postings bulletin board a half a dozen times, each time promising himself he would not look. And he didn't. Not until the seventh time. Then, just to satisfy his own morbid curiosity, he quickly scanned the list for churches and businesses in need of traffic control and security for the day.

St. Michael's Church, Janus-Baker wedding, 10:30 a.m. Alexander-Childers wedding, 3:30 p.m. Piper-Matthews wedding, 7:30 p.m. Two officers, two hours for each event.

Georgia would be at the Alexander-Childers wedding in the afternoon. Maybe if he could see Georgia and her boyfriend together, see the way she looked at Trainer, see how the man adored her, he could shake this compulsion to be around Georgia. It was the guilt, he told himself, which triggered a burning need to know how she drank her coffee in the morning, if she left the top off the toothpaste tube, if she painted her toenails.

Telling himself he would bow to Providence and write Georgia Adams out of his life if the jobs were already taken, he walked up to the clerk who assisted in linking off-duty cops with community needs.

"Is St. Michael's all filled up today?" he asked casually.

The young man ran his finger down a grid. "There's one slot left for the evening wedding, seven-thirty. Interested?"

Disappointed beyond words, Ken stood stock still. He'd promised to heed whatever the schedule dictated. He would eventually get Georgia out of his mind. It was just a simple physical attraction, albeit a strong one. Things had worked out for the best—he liked being a bachelor, and she was obviously looking for a more serious relationship.

I try to be an honest person...just as I expect the man I'm seeing to be honest with me.

His track record on honesty took him out of the running anyway, Ken noted wryly.

"Medlock?" the guy asked, waving a hand to recapture his attention. "You want it?"

Disgusted with himself for caring about a woman who'd made it abundantly clear that she wasn't interested in him, he nodded. "I'll take the seven thirty slot. Gratis, for the church."

The clerk pursed his mouth as he made a note. "Mighty nice of you." Then he grinned. "Penance to pay?"

Ken smirked, then grabbed a cup of coffee and returned to his desk, feeling somewhat better. The one upside of not dating Georgia—he would never have to confess that he'd been the man who'd taken the sexual pleasures she'd intended for her boyfriend. He drank deeply of the coffee, still marveling over the week's events. Considering how quickly the situation had snowballed, he should be thanking his lucky stars to have escaped relatively unscathed.

He sat back in his chair with a resigned nod. Yes—lucky, lucky, lucky.

"Hey, Medlock."

Ken turned and jerked his chin up to acknowledge a colleague approaching his desk. "Yeah, Booker?"

"I'm in a bind. I signed up for the three-thirty wedding at St. Michael's, and I just remembered I'm supposed to take my father-in-law golfing. Don't suppose you'd—"

"Absolutely."

16

KEEPING HIS MIND on directing the traffic into the church parking lot from a busy street was difficult when, one, he knew Georgia didn't have a car, and two, he knew that she was planning to arrive early and was undoubtedly already inside. He did, however, keep his eyes peeled for a 1999 black Lexus with a tag number matching the one in his head.

But by the time the wedding was about to be underway, he still hadn't seen one. When the parking lot started crowding, he left the street traffic to the other officer and directed last-minute arrivals into the nearest empty spots. Not the most exciting job, but police work wasn't always exciting. His vital signs did accelerate, however, when he caught a flash of blue darting through the parking lot. Georgia?

He smiled involuntarily. *Georgia.* In a long blue flowery dress that hugged her form, holding an adorable hat on her head so she wouldn't lose it in her haste. She skidded to a halt next to a white car, peered inside, then seemed to be trying every key on a ring. Ken jogged through the rows of cars. "Georgia."

She jerked her head around, and her eyes bugged. "What are you doing here?"

"Volunteer work for the church, ma'am," he said casually, belying the tattoo of his heart at the sight of

her. God, she was beautiful—no, *magnificent* with her
shining hair falling around her shoulders. Just as he'd
imagined. "Is there a problem?"

She pointed to the car. "The bride wrote her own
vows, but left them lying on the front seat. See?"

He nodded.

"But none of these keys seem to work," she said,
trying one or two of them again.

"This is a Toyota," he said. "Those look like Ford
keys to me."

She squinted. "Stacey gave me the wrong keys!"

He shook his head and pulled out a slim tool. "I'm
not supposed to do this for just anybody, but since I
know you and since this is an emergency, I'll make an
exception."

Her grin when the door popped open was reward
enough. "Thank you!" She leaned in to snatch the
sheet of paper, giving him a breath-stealing view of
her legs as the skirt kicked up. She relocked the door,
then swung it shut. "Well...it was nice to see you
again," she said, her voice a bit nervous.

He touched the brim of his hat, then watched until
she disappeared inside the cathedral. His heart
pounded, his body straining forward, compelling him
to go after her. Ken forced himself to return to his job,
but when his colleague said he would take care of
parking the stragglers, Ken removed his hat and ven-
tured inside the cathedral, turning at the staircase and
walking up into the balcony, which was empty save
for the videographer.

He hung back, scouring the audience below. He
found her hat and enjoyed a leisurely look at her as

she peeked over her shoulder toward the entrance of the church in anticipation of the ceremony starting— or maybe of her boyfriend arriving? There was an empty space next to her on the pew, which irritated him immensely. Rob had obviously known about the wedding before Ken had promised for him to "do his best to come." Perhaps the business that had called him out of town had kept him from returning to Birmingham, which still didn't explain why the man hadn't at least called Georgia to say he wouldn't be there.

The organist started playing softly, then the ceremony began. The groomsmen filed in, and Ken studied the groom, who seemed composed except for rocking back and forth on his heels. Ken felt for him and couldn't fathom being in his shoes. Taking a vow to forsake all others for the rest of your life—scary. His parents had beat the odds, going on forty years of marriage, but these days, things were different. *People* were different, not as strong, not as dedicated.

His gaze went back to Georgia and he bit down on the inside of his cheek. Was that why he felt so drawn to the woman? Because she seemed so complex, this woman with the face of an angel whose passionate phone calls would test the devil himself? He squirmed, his stomach burning with want and guilt and some unidentifiable urge to find out what made her tick. A hot flush burned his neck when he realized how he would seem if someone knew what was going on—watching a woman from a balcony with whom he'd been having phone sex without her knowledge.

He swallowed, himself confused by the battery of

emotions pulling at him. He'd never thought of himself as some guy who couldn't take no for an answer. But he had the horrible feeling that something really wonderful was slipping through his fingers. Of all the numbers in Birmingham, why had she called *his* by accident? And why had he responded? And why had they met the following day?

If he gave up now, was he turning his back on fate?

The bridesmaids filed in—he thought one of them was the skinny little friend of Georgia's from the blood drive—and the rest of the wedding party. Then, on the organist's cue, everyone stood as the bride made her way down the aisle. With her back to him, it was easy for Ken to imagine Georgia in the woman's place, approaching the altar with fluid movements. He frowned wryly, projecting Rob's unknown face onto the groom. Was the guy a model type, with spiffy clothes and a fifty-dollar haircut? His ride was expensive enough, and his address put him in a ritzy part of town.

He stole glances at Georgia as the ceremony proceeded. She was rapt, giving solemn attention to the minister's words. Was she foreseeing her own wedding? Would the vows exchanged today either strengthen or weaken her commitment to Robert Trainer?

And the ceremony itself seemed to be going well, with appropriate smiles and nods—until a commotion in the back captured the attention of everyone in the church. Ken couldn't see what was going on directly beneath the balcony, but his instincts kicked in the instant he saw the expressions of panic and horror. He crouched and crept to the front of the balcony, then glanced down through the rails as a man came into view.

"Stacey," the man shouted, his body shaking. "You can't marry him!"

Out of the corner of his eye, Ken noticed the videographer had left his chair and was aiming the camera downward.

"Darren," the bride said, her eyes wide. "You shouldn't be here." Ken could hear the woman's fear.

The groom's face had turned a mottled shade. "How dare you show your face, Haney." Then, as any self-respecting challenged groom would do, he started for the man, his eyes blazing.

But when the man whipped out a knife, the groom stopped short and guests drew back. Involuntarily, Ken's eyes flew to Georgia, who had turned around and looked horrified. Thanks to his crouched position, she hadn't noticed him in the balcony, and neither had anyone else, except for the cameraman.

"Come on," the crazy man shouted at the groom, stabbing the air with his blade. "I told you before that if you're going to marry Stacey, you'll have to get past me first!"

Ken's mind raced, sizing up the situation. The man stood directly beneath him. He could simply announce his presence and draw his weapon, but something about brandishing a gun in church didn't sit well in his gut. His gaze fell upon the metal folding chair the videographer had vacated, and the solution hit him.

GEORGIA'S HEART lodged in her throat. One minute she had pushed aside the hurt of Rob not showing and immersed herself in the unfolding ceremony, and the next a knife-wielding lunatic had taken the church hostage. A memory stirred—Toni mentioning something about Stacey having a creepy ex-boyfriend. She swallowed hard. From his wild-eyed look and the size of that knife, someone was going to get hurt.

A movement in the balcony caught her eye. The videographer was capturing everything on film, and—she gulped—Ken Medlock was holding a folding metal chair over the madman's head. Her heart soared crazily. Then four seconds later, it was all over—the knife fell to the carpet, harmless, and the man lay on his side, moaning, with a bloody gash on his forehead. Several male guests jumped to restrain him.

But at the sight of blood, her own instincts kicked in. She elbowed past the people in her pew and threaded her way through the crowd. "Excuse me, I'm a nurse. Excuse me."

She stepped over the knife, then knelt to scrutinize the man's wound. She sensed, rather than heard, Ken Medlock stride up behind her. The man had such an uncanny knack for being...*around.* And when had she started liking it?

Moving with power and economy of motion, he picked up the knife with a handkerchief and wrapped it. The man emanated quiet authority. "Everyone, step back," he said, waving. He pulled out a set of handcuffs and knelt to the floor. "That means you, too, ma'am," he murmured for her ears only.

She glanced up and was distracted for a split second

by his serious brown eyes. "He might have a concussion."

"He also might have a death wish," he said. "And if he tried to hurt you, I'd have to shoot him. So," he added with a little smile, "please step aside until I can cuff him."

She considered a battle, but was moved by the sincerity of his expression. Ken made her feel... grounded. And secure. And very, very aroused. She swallowed, then moved back in concession.

"Will you hold this, ma'am?" he asked, extending the wrapped knife.

She took it gingerly, surprised by its weight, her mind reeling with other possible outcomes of the situation. An incredibly calm hero, Ken cuffed the man's wrists behind him just as the groom, Neil, walked up with a teary-eyed Stacey.

"Thank you, Officer," Neil said, flushed and flustered, Stacey clinging to his arm.

Georgia stepped forward. "Neil Childers and Stacey Alexander, this is Officer Ken Medlock. Ken is..." She looked at him and her heart jerked crazily. "Ken is a friend."

"You're here with Georgia?" the groom asked.

Ken seemed amused. She was sure her cheeks were scarlet as she added, "He's a friend of Rob's."

"I was handling traffic for the church," Ken offered. "I take it you all know this guy?"

They nodded, their faces grim. "Darren Haney and I dated two years ago," Stacey said.

"I still love you, Stacey," the man moaned, his eyes barely open.

"There's a restraining order on him," Neil said, his mouth twisting, his hold on Stacey tight.

"I'll take care of him," Ken said. "You might have to fill out some paperwork later, but I wouldn't let this creep ruin your day. Can you stand?" he asked the man.

"Don't know," the guy moaned.

"Try," Ken said, pulling him to his feet. He looked at Georgia, then nodded toward the vestibule. "Let's take this out in the hall."

She turned to Stacey and gave her an encouraging smile. "Ken's right. If you allow this jerk to ruin your wedding, he'll win."

The bride exchanged questioning glances with her groom, then smiled and nodded. "We'll wait for you to come back in."

"No," Georgia said, shaking her head. "This could take a while. If I'm not here when you come out, I'll see you at the reception."

"Did Rob make it?" Stacey asked.

"I'm afraid not."

"So bring Officer Medlock. We'll save him a bottle of champagne as a small token of thanks." Neil echoed the invitation.

She hesitated, looking over her shoulder. "I'll ask, b-but he seems to be a very b-busy man." The man would probably have to return to the Bat Cave or something.

"Thanks for helping out with this mess," Stacey said. "We'll look for you both at the country club."

Georgia conjured up a reassuring smile and backed out of the chapel, closing the doors behind her. She stared at the knife she held, still incredulous. At the sound of a moan behind her, she turned, donning her professional face.

Ken had deposited the man on a padded bench, lying on his side. She handed the wrapped knife to Ken, then knelt to check the man's pulse, alertness and the extent of the wound.

"He's going to need a few stitches," she said, straightening. "And his vision seems clear, but he probably should have a CAT scan and spend the night under psych observation."

"What the hell did you drop on my head?" the man mumbled.

"A ton of bricks," Ken snapped, "which is apparently what it takes to get the point across that your old girlfriend doesn't want you in her life." He recited the man his rights, then pulled him to his feet. "I'll take the guy to County—it's the closest facility."

"I'll come with you." Georgia blinked. Had she really said that? "I can help arrange a psych consultation once we get there."

"But you'll miss the wedding."

"I told Stacey and Neil that we'd...that I'd catch up with them later," she said with a shrug, astonished to realize that she'd rather ride in a squad car with this man to a place where she already spent too much time, than attend a wedding for which she'd bought a special outfit.

"Won't your boyfriend miss you?"

"He...couldn't make it." Georgia swallowed. Was it immoral to have a pseudo-date with a man before she'd officially broken off with her boyfriend if the only thing preventing her from breaking off with her boyfriend was that he hadn't shown up?

Ken's smile sent a stab of desire to her midsection that banished her thoughts of Rob, guilty or otherwise. "That's too bad," he said, but his decidedly unsympathetic tone gave her a little thrill.

She followed him to his squad car and slid into the front passenger seat when he opened the door for her. After he took the driver's seat, he radioed an apparent partner on the church grounds and informed him of the situation, then called in his arrest of the man and reported his intention to take him to County. She watched him, fascinated by his efficient speech and his professionalism. Her body fairly hummed with awareness of his proximity, the images of the fantasy shower show she'd given him last night ringing in her mind. The man would be shocked if he knew her thoughts.

He replaced the radio handset and started the car. "I'll drop you off at the reception as soon as we're through. With any luck, you'll be there by the time they cut the cake."

She wet her lips as they pulled out of the church parking lot. "Neil and Stacy asked me to invite you to the reception, said they'd save you a bottle of champagne as a token of their gratitude."

"That's not necessary."

"Ken, someone could have been killed," she murmured, not even attempting to hide her admiration for his quick thinking. "You always seem to know exactly what to do."

His profile seemed more serious than the conversation warranted. "No, believe me, I don't always know what to do. But I'm glad in this instance that no one was seriously injured." Then he gestured to his clothing. "Unfortunately, I can't enjoy that champagne while in uniform." He stopped for a red light.

"Do you live in the vicinity of the Arrowood Country Club?"

"About five minutes from there."

"Then why not stop and change first? I don't mind waiting."

His smile of anticipation sent her pulse skyrocketing. He flipped a switch and his blue lights began flashing, the siren wailing. "But I do."

17

"COME ON UP," Ken said as he shifted into Park. "I'll just be a few minutes and you can say hello to Crash."

Georgia hesitated, then realized she was being silly. Ken Medlock, superhero, was completely trustworthy. Besides, she was curious to see his living space. She followed him up two flights of stairs, then stopped at a nondescript door sporting the number twenty-four. She toyed with her hat, unable to completely ignore the intimate implications of entering his apartment. He, on the other hand, seemed fully at ease as he swung open the door. Georgia wondered briefly if he entertained female guests on a regular basis, then walked inside.

She hadn't expected a tasteful, comfortably decorated, clean apartment with real live plants and pictures of his family studding the built-in bookshelves. "Nice," she said.

"Something to drink?"

She shook her head, suddenly nervous, then fanned herself. "Gee, and I thought *my* apartment was the warmest place in Birmingham."

"Sorry, ma'am," he said with a shrug. "I keep complaining, but this place is still like an oven. By evening it's almost too hot to sleep."

His words sent an erotic thrill through her. Her

thighs quickened. During his bouts of insomnia, did he ever lie awake thinking about her? She couldn't drag her gaze from his thick arms, imagining them around her. The tension hung heavy in the thick air.

"Well," he said, clapping his hands together once. "Why don't you have a seat, and I'll be back in a few." He smiled, then disappeared down a hallway, his shoulders practically spanning its width.

Georgia hugged herself as she wandered around the perimeter of the room, gazing at photos of people who bore such a strong resemblance to Ken, they had to be related. Funny, but now that she thought about it, she couldn't recall ever seeing photos in Rob's house. She hated comparing the two men, but at the moment, it was inevitable.

In the distance a shower kicked on, alerting her to the fact that Ken's muscular body was positioned under running soapy water. Dark skin, dark hair, smooth muscle, long limbs. She pushed away the carnal thoughts and continued her perusal of his apartment.

Instead of leather and glass and chrome, Ken's living room furniture consisted of two big dark-blue denim couches, a blue-and-tan checked recliner, and a low maple coffee table, flanked by a wide-screen TV. She lowered herself to the middle of the nearest couch, her body sighing in appreciation as she sank into cradling cushions. Now *this* was a couch. She closed her eyes and imagined curling up with a bowl of popcorn to watch a movie on the screen, leaning on the shoulder of a large man.

Georgia halted her train of thought, once again

aware of the shower going in the background. She was attracted to the man, but attraction was a long way from sharing a remote control. Ken Medlock had made it very clear he wasn't interested in a serious relationship. And she needed to get this bizarre sexual situation with Rob out of her system, this hormonal high that left her feeling so disoriented. The shower shut off.

She jumped to her feet, suddenly wishing she hadn't come up. Ken was simply too physically intense in her current condition. In fact, maybe Rob would show up at the reception and they could talk, leaving Ken to his own devices. Georgia paced the room, tempted to walk out, having horribly provocative visions of Ken emerging in a towel.

At a noise behind her, she practically jumped out of her skin. She turned to find Crash hobbling toward her on a cast, his head dipping with every arduous step. Touched, she crossed the room and sank to the floor to pet him, remembering the day she'd met Ken. Had it been less than a week? In an amazingly short amount of time he had wormed his way into her schedule and into her mind. If she were the suspicious type, she'd be inclined to think he had planned their meetings, but she knew that notion was absurd. How would Ken have known she would be at the mall, the blood drive, or even the wedding today? Even superheroes didn't have ESP.

She scratched the dog's ears, laughing at her farfetched attempt to find some reason to distrust Ken.

"I think he remembers you from the park," Ken said from the doorway.

She looked up and swallowed hard. He was breath-takingly handsome in dark slacks and a cream-colored shirt. His hair was combed back and lay close to his head. From where she sat, she could detect the woodsy aromas of his cologne and soap. Her senses leapt, her body straining toward his. He walked over and extended his hand to her. His fingers were long and blunt-tipped, sensuous on their own, even if they weren't attached to this man's powerful body.

As if in slow motion, she watched her hand meet his in an intimate clasp, and she allowed him to pull her to her feet. The kiss was inevitable, and perhaps more potent for that reason. Their lips came together with the momentum of two cymbals. She hungrily met his intensity, their bodies molding together. His hands skimmed over her back and she sensed great restraint when he cupped her bottom. He lifted his mouth from hers long enough to rain kisses over her ear, down her neck, whispering her name against her skin. He slid his hands to her rib cage and thumbed the undersides of her breasts through the thin dress. She undulated against him, eliciting a groan.

Crash's sudden bark parted them, and she gasped at the sight of a repairman standing in the door. "Sorry," the guy said sheepishly. "I knocked three times."

Ken put his hands on his hips, his face dark. "Mr. Franks, what can I do for you?"

"Just came to check your air conditioner—every-thing's supposed to be working. But I can come back."

"We were just leaving," Georgia said quickly, gathering her purse and hat. She sidled by the repairman and waited in the hall until Ken emerged, stuffing his wallet into his back pocket and carrying keys. She didn't trust herself to look him in the eye.

"I'm sorry about that, ma'am," he said in a husky voice.

Oh, that lush accent. "It was as much my fault," she said, still shaken by what could have happened. "We both got carried away."

"I meant I'm sorry that we were *interrupted*."

She tingled under his gaze, but offered no comment. Words really weren't necessary in the universal language of animal lust. Her cheeks burned with shame. Had it been only yesterday that she had rebuked his kiss and told him she was involved with someone? What must he think of her?

"Georgia, say something," he said as they descended the stairs.

"We barely know each other," she murmured. "This isn't right."

He stopped midflight. "Give me a chance. I meant it when I said I want to get to know you."

She shook her head. "This isn't a good time for me."

"Because of your boyfriend?" he asked, an unpleasant expression on his face.

Right now her best defense against giving in to her sexual appetite was to keep hot Ken Medlock at arm's length. "Yes, and I'm sorry if I led you to believe anything different." She continued her descent, then waited for him at the bottom of the stairs.

KEN REMAINED SILENT as he joined her at the bottom of the stairs. He had promised himself he would go slow, dammit, but the entire time he was showering, he kept thinking that the most erotic woman he'd ever known was wrapped up in a beautiful, long-haired package, and sat mere steps away in his living room. By the time he rinsed, he'd had to turn the water to icy cold to get his raging libido under control. He thought he'd succeeded until he walked out and saw her sitting on the floor, petting his dog. She'd been laughing, her cheeks glowing and her eyes sparkling. He couldn't help himself.

"Look, maybe this isn't such a good idea," he said, gesturing vaguely between them.

She stared, her blue eyes luminous. "Maybe."

He sighed. "Why don't I drop you off at the reception? I'll give Mr. and Mrs. Childers my regrets when they come down to file the paperwork on that Haney character."

"Don't be silly," she said. "Stacey and Neil would be disappointed if you didn't come. Besides, after what you did today, you should be there."

"Any cop would have done the same thing."

"But it wasn't *any* cop," she said softly. "It was you." She angled her head at him. "You do have the strangest way of showing up when I least expect it. If I didn't know better, I might think that you..."

He swallowed hard. Think that he what? That he knew more about her than she could ever imagine?

She shook her head. "Never mind. Let's go."

Tingling with remorse, he led her to his gray sport utility vehicle. In response to her raised eyebrows, he gave a little laugh. "You didn't think I drove the cruiser all the time, did you?"

"I suppose I did."

"Well, Miss Adams," he drawled, "I'm full of surprises." *And there's one you'd rather not know about, I'm sure.*

At least he'd managed to coax a smile from her, and the tension eased a bit. He unlocked the door and helped her climb inside, setting his jaw when he touched her silky skin. The skirt of her filmy dress hung down, in danger of being caught in the closed door. He picked up the hem of the blue dress and, at a loss, handed it to her. The awkwardness and intimacy of the moment caught at his heart, and a lump of frustration lodged in his throat. He wanted to be with her, to access her mind and her body and her dreams, but the distance she maintained, combined with her loyalty to Robert Trainer, compounded by his guilt over the phone calls...

He stepped back and closed the door, struck by how much he could identify with the lunatic who stormed the church this afternoon. The thought of Georgia marrying someone else before they had a chance to explore the possibility of a relationship made him a little nuts. Ken pulled a hand down over his face. *Get a grip, man—you wouldn't crash the wedding wielding a blade.*

No, but he'd be mighty tempted to make a fool of himself somehow.

Practically shaking from powerlessness, he climbed in the driver's seat and proceeded to act as if everything were normal. It was for the best that nothing had happened upstairs, he reminded himself. Because Robert Trainer would be back soon to lay claim on her heart, and the very least he owed her was a confession that would circumvent a rupture in Georgia and Rob's relationship.

I'll tell her at the reception, he told himself, *after a drink for courage.*

18

"AND A VERY SPECIAL TOAST," Stacey said, lifting her glass, "to our friend and hero, Officer Ken Medlock of the Birmingham City Police Department."

The guests erupted in enthusiastic applause. From across the room, Georgia's heart thumped as he nodded his thanks to the couple, then she drank from her glass. Rob hadn't materialized, so her hope for a buffer from Ken had disintegrated. She'd made herself scarce, moving around the room in an attempt to avoid being alone with Ken. He seemed not to mind, mingling with ease, surrounded by back-patters and hand-shakers who had witnessed the incident at the wedding. And the *women*. Georgia frowned into her half-empty glass. The women were so...*bold* in their body language.

Not that she cared. After all, she'd had her chances. Ken had made no secret of the fact that he wouldn't mind having a physical relationship. And she wanted him, too. But first Rob, now Ken—who would she be lusting after next week? Engaging in sexual games only fed a dangerous appetite. A forbidden boundary was easier to cross the second time, and the activity would have to be progressively more risqué to deliver the same thrill. Where would it end? Not in a committed marriage.

Georgia downed the rest of the champagne and went in search of a phone, thinking she might call Rob to see if they could meet somewhere to talk since she wouldn't get her phone back until tomorrow. She sighed. Although at the time Rob had seemed to enjoy her calls, she'd concluded that he was definitely avoiding her. She wanted to let him off the hook as soon as possible. Literally.

"Georgia."

At the sound of Ken's voice behind her, she closed her eyes briefly, then hurried her steps, scanning the signs on the doors in front of her. When she saw the word *Office* on the second door to the right, she made a beeline for it, despite his rapidly approaching footsteps. His large hand closed around hers on the doorknob, sending her heart into overdrive.

"Georgia," he murmured, "I need to talk to you."

She wished she hadn't drunk that glass of champagne on an empty stomach. She stared at his hand on hers, momentarily mesmerized. "It's not necessary, Ken."

"Believe me, ma'am, it is."

Georgia slowly turned and looked up at the man who was playing havoc with her emotions, and her libido. At soon as she met his gaze, however, she knew she was in trouble. His hand tightened over hers, and his Adam's apple dipped.

I want him, every fiber in her body screamed in unison. His mouth twitched and she felt her lips part. The next instant his mouth was on hers, moving hungrily. He clasped her upper arms with both hands, as if he were afraid she might try to flee. His tongue sought hers, plunging and retreating in a frenzied dance, sending a burn to her thighs. Champagne mingled on their tongues. The friction of skin on skin released the scents of their spicy and sweet colognes. Georgia moaned and jammed her traitorous body against his.

But through the fog of desire, the sound of approaching voices reached her ears. She stiffened and pulled back, recognizing at least one of the voices as a gossipy bridesmaid—if they were seen together, everyone would know, including Rob, that Georgia had been playing Post Office with the man of the hour.

The desperation must have shown on her face, because he said, "In here," and yanked open the door at her back. They ducked inside the dark room and Ken closed the door behind them. They were enveloped in near darkness. The noisy crowd passed by slowly, most of them sounding female, joking and laughing. Someone slipped and almost fell, eliciting a remark about everyone's level of sobriety.

"Did you get a look at that gorgeous cop?" a woman asked. "Whew-we!"

"Wouldn't mind being handcuffed to that guy," another one said, triggering another wave of giggles.

Georgia's entire body pulsed, her senses keened by Ken's kiss and proximity in the darkness. She could hear him breathing, shifting at the group's comments. At last their footsteps and voices faded away.

Relieved that disaster had been avoided, she groped for the doorknob and turned it.

Only it didn't move.

Panic blipped in her heart as she struggled with the doorknob. "It won't open," she hissed.

He made a disbelieving sound. "Let me try."

Georgia yanked her hand back when Ken's touched hers.

He jiggled the knob three times, each attempt more insistent than the last. Then he grunted. "The knob came off."

"Oh, great." Unwilling to accept the possibility that they might be trapped, she turned to inspect their hiding place. Light filtered into the room from a high window on the back wall of the small, narrow room, silhouetting strange shapes that did not resemble an office. She felt along the wall nearest to her for a light switch, but when she found one, the click produced nothing. She flipped it back and forth. Nada. "The light doesn't work," she announced.

"Why were you coming in here in the first place?" he asked, his tone just the tiniest bit accusing.

She bristled. "I was looking for a phone, and I thought the sign on the door said Office." She didn't add that when she heard him behind her, she'd simply wanted to flee, period.

"Looks like some kind of furniture storage closet," he said, his voice angled away from her.

Her eyes had adjusted to the darkness and she could make out old couches, tables, and chairs lining the walls, stacked as high as safety allowed. The air was hot and stale, further proof they were in a stockroom. "There has to be a way out," she said, then took one step and promptly tripped over something.

His foot, she realized when he caught her, his hands touching intimate places. Blatant desire shot through her primed body. In the space of five seconds, the atmosphere changed to libidinous. She could barely see him, could barely make out his silhouette, but the electricity between them practically glowed. She couldn't explain the phenomenon that had materialized between them in scant days, but she was powerless to resist it. His hand sought out her jaw, his fingers brushed the back of her neck, and she knew she was lost.

"Let's find the exit later," he murmured, then kissed her thoroughly.

Like a weary soldier, Georgia almost welcomed the moment of defeat. Her limbs were limp with relief, her mind resigned to the inevitable conclusion of their passion. She threw herself into the kiss—if she was going to relinquish her pride to Ken Medlock, she would do it largely.

19

GEORGIA'S EYES quickly adjusted to the dim lighting, assisted by the glow of his pale shirt. Their kisses grew more feverish and more promising, tongues dancing, teeth clicking. And the *heat*. The stuffy temperature and the sexual energy combined to create moisture at her pulse points. Her senses were sharp-edged, delivering stabs of desire and pleasure that stole her breath. When Georgia could no longer bear the onslaught, she undid the top button on his shirt. The simple act released a torrent of groans and hurried movements until his shirt and the top of her dress lay open to exploring fingers.

His chest was a wall of firm, smooth muscle covered with a triangle of dark hair. She thumbed his flat, taut nipples, wishing she could see his massive body in full light. His heart thudded beneath her palm, as if the man's hard, insistent erection against her stomach wasn't proof enough that he was alive. He caressed her breasts through her sensible bra, her nipples pearled and aching.

"Harder," she whispered, arching her back.

In answer, he unhooked her bra and released her breasts into his hands, then palmed her flesh and rolled the tips until she cried out. Without warning, he lowered his mouth to her nipple, and the remnants of rational thought fled.

"Ahhhh," she whispered, holding his head against her breast, urging him to draw her deeper into his mouth. He flicked his tongue over the sensitive tip, sending sensations exploding over her in waves, carrying her toward the kind of experience she'd only imagined and now wondered if she could withstand.

It was his touch, she decided, that so aroused her. Firm, yet gentle. Powerful, yet restrained. He caressed her as if she were a special treasure that might break if mishandled. And his voice—or rather, his *noises*—sent a jolt to her thighs. Responsive, expressive, bold. She countered with enthusiasm as he transferred his attention to her other breast, and explored any part of him she could reach. Ken lifted his head and stared into her eyes, then guided her quaking hand to his waistband.

Georgia understood. He wanted her, but he wanted the decision to be hers. And somehow, his tentativeness in juxtaposition to his ragged breathing was even more titillating. She dragged in air through her open mouth and slid her fingers beneath his waistband to feel bare skin, emanating warmth, and the wet tip of his arousal. When he moaned, feminine power welled in her chest, giving her the confidence to be daring. She loosened his fly and clasped his thick erection, then leaned into him, pressing her breasts against his chest.

With a long, guttural moan, he cupped her bottom and undulated against her, then pulled up her skirt, one fistful at a time, until his hands tugged at her cotton panties. Her knees weakened when his fingers delved inside and for a split second, she thought she might be too overcome to reciprocate. But long-forbidden instincts kicked in, causing her to stroke his straining staff. Taking her cues from the rumbling noises he emitted, she squeezed her hand down the considerable length with a slow and firm hand, wondering what it would feel like to have him inside her. The mere thought produced more lubrication for his fingers.

"Georgia," he murmured. "I want you now, right here. Please."

"Yes," she whispered, amazed that he didn't know how much she wanted him in return.

He groaned with anticipation, and bunched the skirt of her dress around her waist. Georgia teased them both by rubbing the tip of his manhood against the front of her panties, and was rewarded when his excitement oozed through the thin fabric. From behind, he skimmed her underwear down to her knees, then picked her up and carried her a few feet, settling her on what appeared to be the back of a couch. She clung to his shoulders, feeling the play of his muscles beneath his shirt as he slid her panties down her legs and nudged open her knees. Georgia felt boneless when his shaft trailed along her inner thigh, leaving a path of moisture. In the back of her mind, a tiny alarm sounded, and at the same instant, he hesitated.

"I have protection," he said, his voice low. She felt foolish for not inquiring sooner, and relieved that he shared her concern. The few seconds that passed as he fumbled in his wallet for the condom and rolled it on seemed agonizingly slow. The scent of her own readiness wafted up to tease her nostrils. She urged him to hurry with her hands and her knees, anxious beyond words for their union. At last, he returned to her, wrapping one arm around her back to steady her as he sought entrance to her threshold. Once, twice, three times he probed her wetness, stroking the tip over the heart of her desire until she writhed with expectation. At last he entered her, taking her breath, then filled her slowly.

The rush of adrenaline rose in her body like the mercury of a thermometer thrust into hot water. Inch by inch, she became engorged with white-hot passion, a helpless but intoxicating feeling that made her limbs loose and her mind languid. When they were fully joined, Ken's head fell forward with a great rasping sigh. He kissed her collarbone and murmured erotic words about how good she felt around him, how much he wanted to give her pleasure.

As if the incredible feeling of him pulsing inside her weren't enough, he began to massage her sensitive nub with his thumb in time to short, jolting thrusts that awakened every nerve center. Her climax broke unexpectedly, shattering around her with the force of a sudden thundershower. She groped at his back, crying out as her ecstasy peaked higher and higher, then emitting a long breathless moan as it drained away. His completion came on the heels of hers, a release that wracked his body with powerful spasms that shook the piece of furniture she rested upon. He gasped her name and gathered her to him, holding her as if she were the source of his energy. Georgia felt ut-

terly desirable and fulfilled, and for the first time, un-
derstood the French expression for "orgasm"—*little death*. For one vibrating moment, she wished she
could stay locked in his embrace forever, this man
who had proved reality could surpass decadent fantasies.

But as their breathing quieted and their pulses returned to normal, the outside encroached. Voices rose
and fell, and strains of the live band reached their secret hiding place. Georgia became aware of the sticki-
ness of her skin—perspiration and perfume and sex.
And unused muscles in her hips and legs screamed.
She squirmed and he loosened his grip on her, leaving
kisses on her shoulder before he pulled away.

"Are you okay?" he asked as he set her gently on
the floor.

"Yes." As he removed the condom, the shallow
light from the window danced off his powerful frame,
sending a new, yet familiar wave of awareness
through her. She averted her gaze, then struggled to
right her clothing while struggling to pinpoint her
emotions. She was at a disadvantage because she
wasn't sure how she was supposed to feel. Grateful?
Self-satisfied? Awkward? Somehow she had reached
the ripe old age of thirty without the sexual savvy that
most women took for granted.

Her dress billowed at her waist, her bra and panties
were missing and not visible in the darkness. Ken
pulled up his boxers, but otherwise seemed in no
hurry to redress or even to leave, for that matter.

Not that they could leave, since the doorknob had
fallen off. They were going to have to pound on the

door until someone came. She wiped her hand across her forehead. And how would they explain that they had both wandered into a dark supply closet? She closed her eyes and knelt to find her clothing, trying to cover herself, yet realizing how laughable her modesty must seem at this point. What did he think of her character? Remorse slammed into her with enough power to force her to clutch the back of the couch. What would *she* think of a woman who would have sex in a closet with a man she'd known for mere days?

Not much.

"Here," he said softly, and extended a white object to her in the dark. Her bra.

She turned around to put it on, but he came up behind her and said, "Let me," then fastened the tricky hook for her. After murmuring her thanks, she buttoned her dress hurriedly.

"And here," he said, then extended another white object.

Her panties. Those she could manage on her own. She heard the slide of a zipper and assumed he was repairing his own clothing. Suddenly a dark question darted through her mind: How many closet trysts were on her father's disreputable résumé? Lingering gratification and nagging guilt warred within her. She wouldn't soon forget the physical bliss she'd shared with Ken Medlock, but what kind of place would the world be if everyone went around doing whatever made them feel good? Sex without love was...empty. Disappointing. And, inevitably, destructive.

Her mind reeled. Was it too late to start over with Rob? At least they could build on a foundation of friendship, instead of animal lust. Georgia cast about frantically for a diplomatic way to extricate herself from the lure of Ken Medlock...and her own weakness.

KEN HAD HOPED that their remarkable lovemaking would mark a turning point in their fledgling...*association*, but within seconds Georgia seemed to be slipping out of reach once again.

He cleared his throat, willing words into his head to salvage anything he could out of his abominable lapse in judgment. After all, Georgia wasn't privy to the other facet of their "relationship."

"Georgia, I know what just happened was spontaneous, but I have to admit I've been thinking about it since the first time I saw you." When only silence met his words, he conjured up a small laugh. "In fact, I haven't been able to get you off my mind." He swallowed. "I've been meaning to tell you—"

"Ken, stop." Her voice sounded less than receptive. "I—I don't know what came over me. I know you don't believe this, but I've never done anything like this in my life."

Make love in a closet to a virtual stranger? Or let down your guard and carry your lover with you to the moon?

Her determined sigh was not encouraging. "I think it would be best if we didn't see each other again."

"Georgia—"

"*Ever.* I know these meetings have all been coincidental, but—"

"Georgia—"

"—our paths simply can't keep crossing. There's something—"

"Wonderful?"

"—dangerous about this, this, this—"

"Attraction?"

"Temptation," she amended, and he could hear the frown in her voice. "What just happened was a fluke, a, a, a freak accident."

Apparently the experience hadn't been quite as mindblowing for Georgia. Still, dammit... "Falling in the bathtub and breaking your arm is a freak accident. What happened between us was very deliberate, at least on my part."

She gasped. "You planned this?"

He held up a hand, then realized she probably couldn't see him in the dark. "No, ma'am! I meant once we started kissing..." Ken sighed, knowing he was making an even bigger mess of things, and tried a different tack. "Is this because of your feelings for Trainer?"

She shifted away from him and bumped into something. "Yes," she said finally. "Rob is a good man."

He opened his mouth to tell her what kinds of things Rob was good at, but he stopped short of crossing that line. If Georgia was in love with the man, she probably knew about his past. And if she didn't know, he wouldn't be the one to tell her out of what might be construed as sour grapes.

Besides, he was the first to admit he found the woman irresistible, but what could he really offer her if she broke up with Robbie Boy? He wasn't ready to settle down, to offer her a committed relationship, and certainly not a home in Knox Ridge and a six-figure salary.

"Can we just get out of here, please?" she asked. "I need to find a phone."

Ken recognized yet another opportunity to confess his deception, before she humiliated herself in front of her boyfriend. But imagining the look on her face when she realized the terrible thing he'd done stopped him. And although her hating him would be the best insulation from the woman's unexplainable appeal, he simply couldn't bear the thought of Georgia Adams hating him.

"Sure thing, ma'am."

She sighed. "Must you call me that?"

"What?"

"*Ma'am.*"

He was at a loss. "It bothers you?"

He thought he heard her sniff. "It makes me feel like a...stranger."

"I'm sorry. I was only being respectful."

"Well...don't."

He clamped his mouth shut, sobered by the abrupt change in atmosphere. Misunderstandings. Awkwardness. Complications. All the reasons he'd avoided becoming involved with a woman. And he was foolish to imagine things would be different with Georgia Adams just because his desire for her had reached unbearable proportions.

Feeling worse than lousy, he picked his way back to the door, sized it up, then listened for foot traffic on the other side. Hearing none, he stepped back and, pretending the door was his own backside, kicked it open.

Georgia strode out, leaving behind the scent of her perfume and her body. Ken realized with a sinking feeling that a peaceful sleep did not appear to be anywhere in his near future.

20

THE FOLLOWING DAY was Sunday, so Georgia dragged herself from her disheveled bed and attended late morning Mass, fervently hoping to assuage some of her enormous guilt for her behavior at the wedding reception with Ken. And she did—to a tiny degree. But afterward, during the bus ride to the electronics shop to pick up her phone system, she still battled with inappropriate feelings for the man. The trouble was, her body could not so easily forget the way he had made her come alive. Unbidden, images of their lovemaking would pop into her mind, sending warmth to her cheeks and thighs. And when she thought of Rob, she felt even worse.

After Ken had kicked open the supply closet door, she had run like a spooked doe in search of the office. She'd found it, two doors down, and closed herself off from everyone else, but especially from Ken. And although she had picked up the phone to call Rob at his office where he was probably working late, she hadn't finished dialing, partly because she was still so shaken from the closet incident, she was afraid of what she might say, and partly because Rob deserved more than a hurried call or a quick visit while another man's scent was on her body.

So she'd decided to wait until her head was clear

and her outlook objective, although judging from the way she felt this morning, that could be some time.

She looked out the window, seeing little of the passing landscape. Ken was Catholic. She'd recognized at least a couple of confirmation ceremonies in the family photos in his apartment. Such a nice-looking family, too—big and smiling, their arms around each other. Just the kind of family she wanted to be a part of, wanted to add to. She wondered briefly why Ken didn't seem to want the same thing for himself. Then she swallowed hard. Perhaps he did want a big family someday, just not with the kind of woman whom he could have in a supply closet.

She closed her eyes, telling herself she deserved the self-derision. Ken Medlock hadn't forced her to do anything against her will. It wasn't his fault that she'd been thinking about him, fantasizing about him since they'd first met. It wasn't his fault that he had been an attractive, convenient outlet for her raging hormones. It wasn't his fault that she was seeking something he couldn't offer.

In fact, Ken had been up-front about the fact that he wasn't looking for a commitment. Georgia sighed. No, she couldn't fault the man's honesty.

When she alighted from the bus, she hadn't yet worked out the emotional dilemma in which she had mired herself. The only thing she knew for certain was that she had to sort things out with Rob, and soon. She'd been hurt when he hadn't shown up for the wedding, but on the other hand, he'd warned her that he might have to work late. She couldn't very well blame her ghastly mistake with Ken on Rob not showing up. The men weren't interchangeable—at least not to a woman with an ounce of self-respect.

She sighed as she pushed her way into the store. The customer service line was already backed up, so she had to stand in line for several long moments before she could talk to the same kid who had taken her phone system for repair the previous day.

"Oh, yeah, I remember you," he said with a little smirk. "You were mad because you didn't have any messages."

"Is my phone ready?" she asked through gritted teeth.

"Got it right here," he said, removing a box from a shelf behind him. "The guys and I had a real laugh over this one."

Georgia worked her mouth from side to side. "And why is that?"

"Because," the kid said, plugging her system into an outlet on the counter. "Turns out this recorder is a little quirky. In addition to pressing the '1' button, you got to adjust the volume in one direction or another to get rid of that welcome message."

"What does that mean?"

He gave her a goofy grin and indicated the flashing light. "It means you got tons of messages, lady." He pressed the button and the mechanical voice announced, "You...have...twelve...messages."

"Twelve?" Concern gripped her stomach. What if she'd missed an important call from the hospital, or from her family?

"Message...one...Tuesday...eight...thirty-four...p.m."

"Hey, Georgia, it's Rob. Sounds like you got your new machine. I guess you've already left for the bachelorette party. Wanted to let you know that I've been called to Columbus, Ohio for a meeting—not sure how long I'll be gone. I left a message at the hospital today with someone named Melanie, but I wasn't sure you'd get it. Hope you have a good time tonight with the girls. I'm on a late flight out tonight. I'll call you, okay?"

She frowned. Melanie hadn't given her Rob's message until Wednesday. But then again, maybe he hadn't called the hospital until after she'd left on Tuesday. Wait a minute. Had Rob just said he was flying out Tuesday night? That was weird. He'd been home when she called after coming home from the club.

"Message...two...Wednesday...six...forty...seven...p.m."

"Georgia, hey, it's Rob again. Just wanted to let you know it looks like I'm going to be here for a couple of days. If you need to reach me, call my messaging service at the office. Sorry I missed you." He laughed. "Hope you didn't do something crazy last night after leaving the club."

Georgia frowned. Was Rob so disturbed by her initiating phone sex that he was going to pretend it hadn't even happened? And he must have fallen ill soon after he left the message if he'd made it back to Birmingham by the time she'd called him Wednesday night.

"Message...three...Wednesday...seven...twelve...p.m."

"It's Toni. Just wondering if you've talked to Rob yet about you-know-what and what he had to say. Call me."

Message four was a telemarketer.

"Message...five...Thursday...five...nineteen...p.m."

"Hey, it's Rob. Was hoping to catch you. I see on the news that Birmingham is still under a heat wave, though, so you're probably working overtime in the E.R. I'm still not sure how long I'll be here, but I hope to be back in time to go to Stacey and Neil's wedding. I'll talk to you soon."

Georgia's heart sped up. Something was wrong. Rob didn't sound ill. In fact, he sounded as if he were still in Columbus. She swallowed. But that was impossible—she'd called him at home Wednesday night *and* Thursday night.

"Look, lady," the clerk said. "The line's backing up. Maybe you could finish this at home?"

"Shut up," she said, her mind racing.

Messages six and seven were from telemarketers. Message eight was from the personnel department at the hospital telling her she could pick up a copy of her file update at her earliest convenience—Dr. Story's report on her stint as a veterinarian, no doubt.

Message nine was from her super saying he would try to fix her thermostat, again, on Monday.

"Message...ten...Friday...six...twenty...p.m."

"Hey, Georgia, it's Rob again. Looks like I won't be able to make it back for the wedding. Give Stacey and Neil my best. I'll call you when I get back, probably Sunday afternoon. Looking forward to seeing you."

Her collar had grown moist, and her breathing rapid. The newspapers stacked up on his stoop, his overgrown grass. If she hadn't talked to Rob herself, she'd be tempted to think he was still in Columbus when he made that call. Was he playing some kind of joke? She rubbed one throbbing temple. If he was, it wasn't funny.

"Message...eleven...Friday...ten...sixteen...p.m."

"Georgia, it's Mother. Just wanted to tell you to have a wonderful time at the wedding, dear. And do try to catch the bouquet. Toodleoo."

Georgia closed her eyes briefly, thinking she probably wouldn't tell her mother than when the bouquet was being thrown, she was making animal love in a supply closet to a man who had no intention of ever walking down the aisle.

"Message...twelve...Saturday...eight...forty...a.m."

"It's Rob again." He sounded annoyed, and she wondered where she'd been that she'd missed his call. Probably taking a shower to get ready for the wedding. "I'm starting to get worried since I haven't talked to you for so long. I hope everything's okay."

Her heart lodged firmly in her throat, like that chunk of bagel Ken Medlock had squeezed out of her. *Since I haven't talked to you for so long?*

"Hey, lady," the guy whined. "Give me a break."

"How do you review numbers that are programmed in?" she croaked.

He sighed and pushed a couple of buttons. "You can only see three at a time."

Her gaze flew to the first number she'd programmed: 205-555-6252. It was wrong. Rob's number was 6225. She'd been dialing the wrong...

She covered her mouth when the implication hit her. *Oh...my...God.* She grabbed the counter for support.

"Hey, lady, you okay?"

Georgia shook her head dumbly. She'd been having raw, sensual phone sex with a nameless, faceless stranger. She would, quite possibly, never be okay again.

21

THE BUS RIDE across town was torturous. Georgia kept replaying the events of the past few days in tandem with the messages left on her machine, frantically searching for some explanation other than the one that left a rock in her stomach, but coming up empty-handed. The implication was nauseating: She was dating one man, having phone sex with another, and having real sex with a third.

When had her life taken such a bizarre twist?

She closed her eyes briefly. When she'd allowed physical needs to override her good judgment. One thing was certain—she had to get to Rob's before he found the little note she'd left about having X-rated fun on the phone. After that, she'd take it one step at a time, assuming there was actually a way to extricate herself from the mess she'd created.

So, dragging the box containing her phone system, she disembarked from the bus and practically trotted the distance to Rob's home. When she saw the local Sunday paper and the *New York Times* lying rolled up on the stoop, she was torn between relief that he hadn't arrived home and dismay that her suspicions were beginning to look horrifically correct.

She set down her box, scooped up the papers, and fished the door key from her wallet with a hand that shook uncontrollably. She dropped the key altogether when a car horn sounded from the street. When she turned, her heart dove. Rob's black Lexus rolled into the driveway. The note—she had to get the note. The garage door went up and he guided the car inside. She scrambled for the key, thinking she could still beat him to the kitchen even if he entered the house through the mud room. At last she seized the key, then shoved it home and turned it. The dead bolt gave, and she practically fell inside. When she slid into the kitchen, Rob had already spotted her note and was two steps away. She darted in front of him and yanked it out of reach, then gave him a cheerful smile.

"Welcome home."

"Thanks." He gave her a quick peck on the mouth, then his smooth face creased into a quizzical frown. "What's that?"

"What?"

"That piece of paper you just grabbed."

She looked down at her hand. "Oh. This is nothing—just a note I left when I came over the other day to, um, bring in your newspapers."

"Oh. So you did get my messages?"

"Um, yes. Yes, I did."

He smiled. "I was beginning to think there was something wrong with your machine because I couldn't catch you."

Nothing wrong with my machine, just me, she thought miserably. She had hoped for some spark, some sense of excitement at the sight of Rob, but she was merely...sad. Sad that she and Rob both maintained a physical and emotional distance that neither seemed able to pierce, and neither seemed willing to shed. And perhaps neither was to blame—they simply weren't compatible on any level of intensity. In the few days that had passed since she'd last seen him, she had changed too much, had learned things about herself that would alarm and perhaps disgust someone as placid and passionless as Rob Trainer. Still, she owed him some sort of explanation.

"Is something wrong?" he asked. "You look... worried."

The understatement of the year. "Rob, we need to talk."

"Is that Stacey and Neil's wedding?" he blurted, distracted by the Sunday paper that had fallen open on the counter where she'd tossed it. *Local Cop Saves the Wedding Day*. Sure enough, a photo series obviously taken from video stills showed Officer Ken Medlock holding a folding chair over the balcony, the madman being struck down—especially effective since his knife had been knocked from his hand and hung in midair—and another of Ken handcuffing the man. Georgia sighed. Was she destined to be reminded of the man at every turn?

"Yes," she said. "It was a bit of a commotion, but everyone was fine. Um, your friend Ken Medlock saved the day."

His pleasant face folded. "My friend?"

"Officer Ken Medlock. You know, the cop from the gym. I've, um, run into him a few times over the past few days."

Rob squinted at her and his Adam's apple bobbed.

"Your face is all red. Does this have something to do with the cop?"

She tried to will away the flush and clasped her hands together to keep from fidgeting. "Well—"

"Georgia."

She glanced up at his sharp tone, stunned that his expression was a cross between fury and panic.

"I don't appreciate anyone poking around in my past," he said quietly.

Her mouth opened and she shook her head. "But I wasn't—"

"I don't know anyone by the name of Ken Medlock, and I certainly don't know any city cops."

"But he said—"

"I made a mistake," Rob said, smacking his hand on the counter, causing her to jump. "And I served my time."

Georgia backed up a step, stunned by his mood change and the turn of the conversation. He had a record? "Why didn't you tell me?" she asked with as much calm as she could muster.

"Because my past is none of your business," he bit out. "It was one lousy charge of embezzlement—a few thousand dollars to pay off some debts. What is it to you?"

She felt like a fool. Rob had no intention of getting close to her, and deep down, she'd known it from the beginning. She'd perpetuated the relationship because it was safe, because it didn't require her to extend herself or be vulnerable in return. Rob was the kind of man she thought would provide the most stable home for a family, someone to...offset her urges?

"You're right," she murmured. "It's none of my business. I'm leaving."

"Georgia, wait," he said, his expression contrite. "I'm sorry to go off on you like that." He sighed. "It's just not working between us, you know?"

She nodded. "I know."

"But you're such a nice person."

"Thanks, Rob. I feel the same way about you."

"I'd appreciate it if you didn't say anything to anyone about that mess back in Ohio." He smiled sheepishly, and she wondered what she had ever seen in the man.

"I won't." She laid the door key on the counter, then walked out, nearly tripping over the box that held her phone system. All she wanted to do was go home, lie on her hard couch, and have a good, long cry.

Toni sat in the hard chair that matched the hard couch. "I don't believe it. I just don't believe it."

Georgia lay with her hand over her forehead. "Believe it."

"And you have no idea who this guy is?"

"None whatsoever."

"Wow. How romantic."

She sighed. "I was thinking it was more like something in *Penthouse* Forum."

"Your life is so exciting. Oh! This is just like my situation with Dr. Baxter—he doesn't know who I am, either, but there's this connection, you know?"

"Toni, I don't think it's the same thing at all."

"Well, do you want to find out who this guy is?"

She turned her head. "Of course I do. He could be

some psycho with caller ID who knows my name and number."

"Or some gorgeous single hunk."

"Toni, you're nuts. He's probably married and has kids." Like her father.

"Why don't you call the number now?"

Georgia frowned. "Now?"

"Maybe the guy works during the day and he'll have his machine on, or someone else will answer."

She chewed on the inside of her cheek. "I don't think I want to call the number again."

"I'll do it from my cell phone," Toni offered, reaching for her purse.

Georgia recited the number and sat up as Toni punched it in. "It's ringing," she said excitedly, then handed the phone to Georgia.

She swallowed past the lump in her throat, praying a wife or child wouldn't answer. But after the fourth ring, a voice recorder kicked on with a generic mechanical message. She hung up with a sigh. "Maybe I should just chalk it up to a bad experience. After all, the guy hasn't called me back."

"But that doesn't mean he won't," Toni said. "He could be outside right now, going through your trash, looking for the hair from your brush."

"Oh, now that makes me feel good."

Toni snapped her fingers. "I've got it! A friend of mine told me the police have those reverse phone indexes—they can look up names by the number."

"And what good does that do me?"

"All you have to do is ask that big strapping Officer

Medlock to do you a favor. Besides," she wagged her eyebrows, "now that Rob is out of the picture—"

"Don't even say it," Georgia said, holding up her hand. She had enough problems on her plate without getting involved with Ken Medlock. She blinked back hot tears. How utterly stupid she'd been—anyone could have walked in on them, anyone could have seen them coming out of that room. Besides, she'd traded twenty minutes of passion for a lifetime of regret—regret because she knew if given the opportunity, she'd probably do it again. And again. And again.

"You have to admit, he's a hottie," Toni pressed. "When he came charging into the back of the church wearing that uniform, I swear half the women in the church swooned. Rebecca Dooley had her eye on him at the reception, but he disappeared right after the toast."

"Really?" Georgia pressed her palms into her eyes, but snatches of his lovemaking remained so vivid in her mind, her womb clenched and her thighs tingled. God help her, even with everything else going on, she couldn't stop thinking about the man—a clue as to how dangerous he was to her mental well-being.

"He's *interested*, Georgia. You're crazy if you don't go out with him."

"He's a player, Toni. The man told me himself he's not interested in settling down."

"So? You don't have to marry him. Just have a little fun."

She smiled wryly to herself. Just have a little fun? Ken Medlock would be too easy to fall for, and too hard to forget. She had already set into motion events that might haunt her for years. She'd learned her lesson about indulging her darker urges, no matter how tempting.

Toni sighed. "You should go see him, you know. You wouldn't have to give him all the details, just make up something. He owes you one after almost getting you fired and all."

Actually, after their encounter in the closet, they were even, she conceded silently. She'd felt so ashamed for her behavior that she'd even lashed out at him for calling her "ma'am."

I'm sorry. I was only being respectful.

Considering what she had just allowed to transpire, his respectfulness had grated at the time.

Georgia closed her eyes and sighed. The man had only been trying to make the best out of a horribly awkward situation. And Toni was right—the quickest way to find the identity of the guy on the other end of the phone line and to have peace of mind was to go to Ken. She wouldn't have to give him all the details, and she believed he would be discreet. Besides, as far as he knew, she was still dating Rob, so he wouldn't pressure her to see him, not after their discussion in the closet. Indeed, asking for his help would give them a chance to ease the awkwardness of their last parting. And once Ken told her the name of the man who belonged to that phone number, she would be able to put the chaos of the past week to rest.

22

KEN JUMPED UP when the hot coffee hit his lap. "Dammit!" He stamped around, swiping at the wetness with a paper towel, then glared at his partner Klone. "What are you looking at?"

From his adjacent desk, Klone lifted an eyebrow. "I'm wondering when someone kidnapped my sweet-tempered partner and left a wounded bear in his place."

He frowned as he dropped back into his seat. "Just having a bad day, that's all."

Klone gestured to the pile of cards and letters that had accumulated throughout the day. "Yeah, it's rough being a freaking hero, ain't it?"

Ken scoffed in the direction of the mail. "My home phone has been ringing off the damn hook." Everyone who had his number had called—his mother, his sisters, his brother, his neighbors, his buddies—everyone except Georgia. And he'd only flipped through the silly cards today on the slim chance that Georgia had sent him a note of some kind.

Why she would, he had no idea, but a man could hope. Since Saturday, he had thought of little but Georgia, wondering if Trainer had made it home, and if she'd discovered she hadn't been talking to her boyfriend when she'd...

Ken rubbed his fists over his scratchy eyes. He hadn't slept much at all the past two nights, and the strong coffee meant to clear his head was making him irritable.

Then he frowned. Okay, his conscience was making him irritable. One foolish split-second decision to self-ishly seize the moment had snowballed into an emotional quagmire. Worse, he'd passed up several chances to stop the madness and/or confess the truth. The fact that he'd used a nice, innocent woman led to a troubling state of mind—he was disappointed in himself. Before now he'd always thought of himself as a person of decent character, but one of his father's fa-vorite sayings kept circling in his mind: *It's easy to be a good person if your character is never tested.*

Boy oh boy, he'd failed miserably. He sighed. The answer was painful, but simple: He had to tell Georgia the truth, no matter the consequences.

"Woman trouble?" Klone asked, clamping him on the shoulder.

He looked up. "What the devil makes you think that?"

"Takes a lot to get you discombobulated."

Ken scowled. "Well, it's not a woman." It was what he'd done to her.

Klone shook his head. "You're a bad liar, son."

No, he was a great liar—that was the problem.

"It's that little slip of a nurse who was in here the other day, ain't it?"

"No."

"The one you rounded up all the guys for the blood bank to impress."

"No."

"Well, at least she's an upstanding woman. Might make an honest man out of you."

Ken smacked his hand on the desk. "Dammit, Klone, I'm telling you it's not—" He stopped when he spotted none other than Georgia Adams being led toward his office. A goofy grin hung itself on his face. He stood so abruptly his chair went flying backward. And his stupid heart rolled over like a trained pet.

"Well, lookie there," Klone drawled. "If it ain't the woman who don't have you tied up in knots."

Ken watched her. Her heavy-lidded smoky gaze, the way she moved, the whole of her made his breath catch in his throat. In that moment, he had a revelation. From now on, he would refer to his life in two phases: before he met Georgia Adams, and after.

"Wonder what she wants," Klone muttered.

He didn't care, as long as she was here. One thing he knew for certain—if Rob Trainer wanted Georgia, the man was in for the fight of his life. Unable to stop himself, he met her halfway, grinning like a dolt. "Hi."

"Hi." She smiled and blushed, a great sign that bolstered his mood higher. His imagination took flight. She had broken off with Rob. She was hoping they could get together for a movie or something. She wasn't busy for the next forty years or so. She wouldn't mind having a gimpy dog underfoot.

"I brought the pictures of Crash," she said, handing him an envelope.

"Oh. Thanks."

"And I need a favor," she said, her blue eyes wide and earnest.

He focused on not touching her, not here in front of everyone. "Anything," he said, and meant it. "Come on back to my desk." He pointed the way, then walked behind her a half step, throwing Klone a warning glare as Georgia sat down. The man pursed his mouth and turned back to his own paperwork.

Ken tried not to be distracted by her slim thighs as she crossed her legs. The simple, close-fitting khaki shorts hugged her figure, bringing back gut-clutching memories of her legs around his waist. He cleared his throat. "What can I help you with, Georgia?"

She removed a slip of paper from her purse and extended it to him. "Can you tell me the name of the person who has this local number?"

His heart stopped at the sight of his own phone number written in dainty little numbers, so innocent. Unable to take the slip of paper, he simply stared at it, willing it to go away. His brain clogged, and his vision blurred. What had seemed like the right decision a few moments ago now faded in the wake of losing the chance to win her over.

"Why do you need it?" he heard himself ask in an amazingly calm voice.

Her coloring rose and she squirmed. "Well, I'd rather not go into too much detail. The number has been called from my phone, and I'm just curious as to who is on the other end, that's all." But her smile didn't reach her eyes.

Ken didn't know what to do, so he stalled. "Someone has been using your phone without your permission?"

"N-no."

"So you made the calls."

"Yes, but I dialed the wrong number—this number."

Picking up on her discomfort, he decided that if he pushed her, she might change her mind about wanting the name. "If it was the wrong number, why do you need the name?"

"B-because," she said softly, "I, um, divulged information to this man which was rather personal."

"Information that was meant for someone else?" he pressed.

"Um, yes."

"What purpose would be served by finding this person?"

She averted her eyes and rolled her shoulders. "I'm not sure—"

"Hey, Ken," Klone called from his desk a few feet away, a phone in the crook of his shoulder. "There's a lady up front who wants to talk to you about a lost dog."

A sliver of disappointment cut into him. That mutt was starting to grow on him, and he was halfway hoping no one claimed him. At the same time, he knew someone was probably worried to death about the poor pooch. And he recognized the opportunity to collect his jumbled thoughts. He gave Georgia an apologetic glance. "Do you mind?"

"No, go ahead," she said, standing. "I think I've

changed my mind anyway. It's silly, really. I'm sure the man dismissed the incident."

No, he didn't dismiss it, he wanted to say. *He loved it. He might even love you.* Ken straightened, shocked by the direction of his guilty thoughts. "I'm due a break. What would you say to grabbing a bite to eat? I'd like to talk to you, in private." She looked as if she were going to say no, so he added, "Please?"

At last she smiled and nodded. "Okay, but just for a little while."

He grinned. "Great. Sit tight and I'll be right back to get you, okay?"

She nodded and sank back into the chair, looking small and gorgeous and...perfect. He couldn't tell her now, not when that tentative look was starting to leave her eyes. *She'll never know I was the man she was talking to,* he told himself. *And it's better for both of us.*

"I'll hurry," he said, as eager to return as a boomerang.

GEORGIA FELT CONSPICUOUS sitting in Ken's big chair. She glanced around his work environment, thinking it wasn't so different from her own—lots of shared space, a smidgen of private space, loads of camaraderie, a flurry of constant activity. She liked it.

And she liked Ken. A lot. Maybe she had misjudged him. Maybe he wasn't the ladies' man he was reputed to be. Maybe that closet episode was as remarkable for him as it had been for her. Maybe the odd coincidences of their paths crossing meant something special was supposed to happen between them.

She sighed, remembering the reason she'd come to

the station in the first place. Ken was right. What would she do with the information if she did get the guy's name? Call him and demand that he not tell anyone that she preferred sleeping in the nude? Chances were the man had an interest in remaining anonymous, and she would probably never know his identity. She conceded, however, that months might pass before she stopped glancing at men on the bus and wondering if *he* were the one.

Whoever the guy was, he was probably having a belly laugh over the desperate woman who had to make the first move with her boyfriend, and who was so distracted she couldn't even tell that the person on the other end wasn't him. She burned with humiliation when she thought of the things she'd told him— intimate things she thought she was sharing with a man who cared about her. If the guy had caller ID, he knew her name. Had he told all of his buddies? Was her name being distributed on the Internet? *For a good time, Georgia Adams will call* you.

"Howdy," said a lumpy-looking middle-aged man who came over to pick up a form from Ken's cluttered desk. "I'm Klone."

"I'm Georgia Adams," she murmured. "You're Ken's partner, aren't you?"

"That I am."

From the twinkle in the man's eyes, she knew he was fond of Ken. "He's spoken of you," she said.

He smiled again. "And I know all about you, too."

She blinked. "Ken has mentioned me?"

"Oh, sure, Ken has mentioned you to just about anyone who'll listen." He leaned forward and dipped his chin. "He thinks you're just about the hottest number in Birmingham."

Guilty heat flooded her face.

A young man walked up, his hands full. "Another stack of cards for Ken," he said, adding to the pile of envelopes overflowing the small desk. He held up a postcard. "As if the man didn't have enough women chasing him, he has to go and make the front page of the paper. Listen to this: 'You can handcuff me to your bed any time. Call me, Barbie.'" He rolled his eyes.

The officers in the vicinity laughed, and Georgia felt uneasy. The man obviously had his pick of women to coax into a closet. Why would he be interested in her?

Klone picked up the slip of paper she'd left lying on Ken's desk and to her surprise, winked broadly as he handed it back to her. "Ken really should get business cards for as often as he's probably passed out this number."

Georgia's mind flooded with confusion. She tried to smile. "Do you...recognize this phone number?"

Klone glanced at the paper again. "Yep—555-6252—I've sure as hell dialed it enough. It's Ken's home number."

The floor fell out from under her feet, leaving her in a free fall. A week's worth of seemingly disjointed events fell into place with mocking ease, like a preschooler's puzzle. Running into him at the hospital, then seemingly at every turn. At the hospital, at the mall, at the blood bank, at the church. He'd looked her up and hunted her down. He'd played her for a fool, an *easy* fool. Scoring in the supply closet. She covered her mouth with her hand to keep from crying out.

"Is something wrong?" the man asked.

Oh, sure, Ken has mentioned you to just about anyone who'll listen. He thinks you're just about the hottest number in Birmingham.

Georgia lunged to her feet, stumbling backward before she gained her footing. Bile rose in her mouth. "I...have to go," she whispered, then ran blindly toward the exit.

KEN WAS WHISTLING when he walked back to his desk. The woman's lost dog wasn't Crash, and Georgia was waiting for hi—

He frowned at the empty chair, then panned the adjacent area looking for her. "Klone," he called, threading his way through people to their desk area. "Where's Georgia?"

The older man shrugged. "Took off, like someone set her on fire."

"Just like that?" He narrowed his eyes. "Did you say something to her?"

"Maybe a little good-hearted teasing, but nothing to send her off like that. I think she's a little touched in the head."

"You're the only one here touched in the head. Think, man. You had to have said something that upset her."

The man shook his head. "Nope. Cal over there delivered some more mail from your fan club and was cutting up about what a lady killer you are. Then I cracked a joke about you making up business cards so you wouldn't have to write down your phone number so often."

Dread pooled at the top of his head and oozed downward. "My phone number?"

"Yeah, she had it written on a piece of paper. Guess you wore her down for a date?"

He leaned forward and gripped the sides of his desk. "You told her that was *my* phone number written on that piece of paper?"

"Well, wasn't it?"

Ken closed his eyes and swallowed.

"What the hell is going on?" Klone asked.

He straightened. "I'm going on break."

"For how long?"

"I don't know."

Ken jogged to the front of the building and burst through the double doors. A hundred feet away, a city bus had stopped for passengers. He caught the flash of a pink blouse and took off sprinting. But the bus lumbered into motion and pulled away just as he ran up next to it. He searched the windows for her face and when he saw her, his stride broke. Tears streaked her face and she looked at him with such loathing, he was rooted to the spot. He opened his mouth, but knew it was too late for words.

He watched the bus carry her away from him and felt like the piece of trash that lay on the sidewalk at his feet.

23

"MAYBE I HOULD MOVE to Denver," Georgia said, wiping her nose. "I'm sure my brother-in-law would help me find a job." She tossed the tissue into the garbage can next to the kitchen sink, and grabbed a fresh one for a hearty blow.

For the first time since Georgia had known her, Toni was speechless, and had been since she'd divulged the shocking truth. Her friend could only shake her head, which Georgia feared would come off from all the wagging.

"Jesus, Toni, say something."

"I'll help you load the moving van."

Georgia's face crumpled as a new wave of stinging tears assailed her. Her shoulders shook from abject shame and humiliation and something worse—disappointment. Disappointment that she had started to think that Ken Medlock was a decent guy, maybe even someone she could love. Maybe even someone who could love her back.

Her heart shivered, overcome with sadness.

Toni hugged her, and allowed her to cry for several long moments, then led her to a kitchen chair. "You sit while I fix us something cold to drink. Hmm. Did you know your refrigerator light is burned out?"

Georgia nodded, then sat down heavily. At least the

super had honored his word and fixed her programmable thermostat while she was at work this morning. Wouldn't it be nice if she could simply reprogram her heart? Although, with her technical ineptness, she'd probably wind up losing a kidney.

She held her head in her hands, picturing Ken running next to the bus, looking for her. What had driven him to come after her—guilt over his behavior? Fear that she might report him to a superior? Certainly not concern for how she felt being manipulated like a hunk of warm wax.

The things she'd said to him... *Oh, God.*

The phone rang, sending Georgia's heart into her throat. She and Toni exchanged looks, but she allowed it to ring two, three, four times and roll over to the machine. Her own voice invited the caller to leave a brief message, then a beep sounded.

"Georgia, this is Ken." His loud, deep voice penetrated the air, the microphone broadcasting in stereo sound.

Her sob turned into a hiccup. How dare he call her?

"If you're there, please pick up."

She sat rooted to her chair, her eyes narrowed at the machine.

He sighed. "Look, I don't blame you for never wanting to talk to me again. I can imagine what you must think of me. I just wanted to say that...I'm sorry. I'm so sorry, Georgia. It started out as innocent fun, and it got out of hand. Once I got to know you, I wanted to tell you. I *tried* to tell you at the reception before we...well, you know."

Toni shot her a raised-eyebrow look. Georgia closed her eyes.

"I was even trying to think of a way to tell you today—that's why I wanted us to be alone." He grunted. "Although I can't honestly say I would have, because things seemed to be going well between us, and I was hoping..."

Georgia opened one eye. He was hoping?

"I was hoping..."

She opened the other eye. He was hoping?

"I was hoping you wouldn't hate me."

She frowned. Too late.

"I'm sorry I deceived you, but I swear, I meant everything I said when we were on the phone."

Toni pursed her mouth.

After a pause, he said. "Well, I won't bother you again. I just couldn't let things end like this. I'm sorry, Georgia."

The call disconnected and the beep sounded again. She wiped her eyes. Her face and body ached with pent-up emotion.

Toni set two glasses of pink lemonade on the table and sat down in an adjacent chair. "Well," she said, lifting hers for a drink.

Georgia sniffed. "Well, what?"

"Well, he sounded apologetic."

She scoffed. "He's sorry, all right—sorry he got caught."

Toni sipped, then asked, "What was all that about the you-know at the reception?"

She stared into her glass, but knew her face was just about as pink as her drink.

"Georgia?"

She sighed. "We made out in a storage closet."

"Ah. So that's where he disappeared to. I thought you were leaving to call Rob."

"I was," she said miserably. "But he followed me, then we kissed, then we heard someone coming, so we hid in a closet, then one thing led to another." She covered her mouth and breathed through her fingers. "And the whole time, he knew."

Toni put her hand over Georgia's on the table. "Okay, let's break this down. You thought you were calling Rob and dialed Ken's number by mistake."

"Right."

"Then the next day, you met Ken when he came into the E.R. with a dog."

"Right."

"Well, he couldn't have very well planned to hit a dog just to bring him in."

She shook her head. "No, Ken wouldn't do something like that. It was coincidental, I'm sure."

"But when he found out your name, he figured out who you were?"

Georgia bit on her lower lip, trying to remember their initial introduction. "He asked me if he knew me from somewhere, then said he knew a guy named Rob who dated a woman named Georgia, and I asked him if he was talking about Rob Trainer."

"And he said yes?"

She nodded, then her eyes went wide. "I must have called him Rob on the phone. He made up the part about knowing a Rob just to see if I was the person who had called him!"

Toni nodded. "Sounds reasonable."

Georgia smacked herself on the forehead. "The note."

"What note?"

"When I was leaving the hospital that day, Melanie gave me a note and told me that Rob had been called out of town."

"And Ken overheard this conversation?"

She nodded.

"So he knew Rob was out of the picture for a few days."

"But he couldn't have known that Rob wouldn't call, or that my message recorder was fouled up."

Toni shrugged. "I guess he figured he'd take his chances." She grinned. "You must be good."

Georgia blushed. *They* had been good.

"I just think it's amazing that you were torn over breaking up with Rob because you felt like you guys were making headway, when the guy you were really making headway with was the same guy you were lusting and feeling guilty about."

She squinted. "I think I followed that."

"You get the gist."

Georgia sipped her lemonade. "Mmm. What did you put in here?"

"Rum," Toni said, pointing to the bottle on the counter. "Take a big drink. What was Ken referring to when he said he meant everything he said when you all were on the phone?"

She froze.

"What?"

"Well, there was one night—no, never mind."

."What, Georgia?"

"There was one night when I thought Rob was going to tell me that he loved me, and I got all panicky."

"You mean *Ken* was going to tell you."

"Well, at the time I thought it was Rob."

"So why did you get all panicky?"

She swallowed a mouthful of spiked lemonade. "Because...I suppose I knew that I didn't love Rob."

"Because?"

"Because..." She glanced at her friend and sighed. "Because I was falling for Ken."

Toni squeezed her hand. "Then don't you see? This is perfect! He likes you, and you like him."

She shook her head and groaned. "But how could I? I barely know the man."

"So? You knew Rob for ten months and that didn't help. You didn't even know he had a criminal record, for heaven's sake."

But Ken probably did, which could explain why he'd kept asking her about her relationship with Rob. She frowned. There was something honorable buried in the fact that he could have told her, but hadn't, although she couldn't sort it all out at the moment.

"But the man played me for a fool. He knows things about me. Private things."

"And you know private things about him."

True, she conceded. And some deep dark part of her was slightly relieved that at least a third man hadn't been involved in her web of lust. At least she'd had phone sex with a man that she—what?

Cared about? Maybe.

But trusted? Never.

24

KEN STOPPED in front of the E.R. doors to County and rubbed his scratchy eyes. He hadn't gotten a wink of sleep last night, worrying about Georgia, stewing in the misery of what he'd done to her.

Interspersed among the despair, of course, were more positive images. Of her at the mall, flustered after their encounter, laden with shopping bags. Of her taking his blood, then goading him into rallying his buddies for a good cause. Of their kiss in the park, when she'd tasted like sweet relish and fresh air. Of her running through the church parking lot in that filmy blue dress. Of her sitting on the floor of his living room, playing with Crash. Of their frenzied lovemaking in the dark closet. Of the light of possibilities in her amazing blue eyes when she'd come to the station yesterday seeking his help, never imagining he was the guilty party. Some superhero.

Last night had crawled by, and since Franks had fixed the air conditioning unit, he couldn't blame the temperature. But he'd discovered that the fires of regret could be just as hot as the Southern sun.

Ken took a deep breath for courage. He simply had to see her again, and although he knew her address, he didn't feel comfortable going to her apartment. The woman was already spooked. And the fact that Robert

Trainer hadn't contacted him probably meant she hadn't told her boyfriend the truth, which made him feel even worse.

The doors opened automatically, and he walked inside, panning the area for a glimpse of Georgia. His heart pounded in his ears.

"May I help you, Officer?" a woman at the admissions desk asked.

"Nurse Georgia Adams—is she working today?"

The woman pointed behind him.

Ken turned to see Georgia staring at him, hugging herself. At the sight of her sad, heavy eyes, he practically tore the hat he was holding in two. After a hard swallow, he walked toward her and stopped. "Georgia—"

"Why are you here?"

Mindful of the ears all around them, he grasped at the only straw at his disposal. "To have you check my blood pressure." He took the fact that she didn't throw something at him as a good sign and added, "Just as you ordered."

"Anyone can take it," she murmured.

"Please."

She wet her lips, then inhaled and said, "Wendy, I'll be in exam room three."

Her voice was tight, and her body language closed as he followed her. Ken remembered the time he and Klone had entered an apartment building where an armed man had holed up after a bank robbery. What could it mean that he was more afraid now than he'd been then? And that the image of Georgia's tear-streaked face in the bus window had wounded him more than the lead he'd taken in the shoulder when they had rushed the criminal?

"Have a seat," she said, sweeping her arm toward a sterile chair. He recognized the room as the same one in which she'd bandaged Crash. Ken closed the door behind them, then lowered himself onto the small chair.

"Georgia—"

"Your arm, please," she said, holding out a blood pressure cuff.

He lifted his arm so she could fasten it tightly. She refused to look at him as she squeezed the plastic bulb that forced air into the cuff around his arm. When the pressure bordered on pain, she released the air, watching the gauge.

"It's still a little on the high side, but within normal range for a man of your size." She peeled off the device with a rip of Velcro.

"Georgia." He curled his fingers around her wrist loosely.

She looked at him, her eyes moist, then jerked away. "Get out."

He lifted his hands, then stood slowly. "I just wanted to tell you that I'm sorry."

"So you said in your phone message."

"I wanted to tell you in person."

"I thought my lack of response would make it clear that I didn't want to talk to you and certainly didn't want to see you. But," she said, her eyes pooling, her voice straining, "maybe you're the kind of guy who has to be hit with a ton of bricks to get the message."

Her words cut him like the blade of the madman

who had rushed the church. She was right. He was no better than that obsessed jerk who wouldn't take no for an answer. That fool was probably also convinced that he was in love.

Ken stopped, mostly because his heartbeat had paused. It was a fair response from his body considering the revelation that had arrested his brain: He loved her.

"Don't make me call security," she whispered, then backed up against the exam table behind her. A solitary tear traveled down her cheek.

He'd never felt more helpless in all of his life. He was the biggest fool in Birmingham, maybe in the entire southeastern United States. A woman like Georgia Adams came along once in a lifetime—maybe. How ironic that he'd spent most of his adult life trying to figure out how to stay out of a relationship, and just when he was thinking about the possibility of maybe sort of trying to picture himself with one woman, she'd slipped through his fingers. No, he'd pushed her away with his games of deceit and manipulation. He didn't blame her for hating him.

He strode out of the room as fast as his long legs would take him. Away from Georgia, so he couldn't hurt her anymore. One thing he knew for certain: She was the hardest lesson he'd ever learned.

Ken had jammed his hat on his head and was nearly out the door when he heard a man calling, "Officer Medlock!"

He turned and conjured up a pleasant expression. "Hello, Dr. Story. Nice to see you again."

The little man looked like an opossum, but he had

an excellent reputation in the city. "I just wanted to let you know that after our conversation Saturday morning, I decided to remove the reprimand from Nurse Adams's file."

"Thank you," he said, truly relieved at the one bit of good news.

"From your explanation, I realize she did her best to circumvent the situation."

But as usual, Ken thought, he had pushed until he'd gotten his way, and in the process, had jeopardized the woman's job. What a selfish bastard he'd become. Never opening himself to other people, never considering how his actions might affect others, never putting his own emotions on the line.

"My wife runs the city blood bank," Dr. Story said. "I heard about you rallying your fellow officers to build the reserves. We're indebted to you, Officer Medlock. If there's ever anything I can do for you, just ask."

Ken started to shake his head, then recalled his emotions after the church incident. He'd acknowledged that he could almost identify with the lunatic because if he were about to lose Georgia, he wouldn't wield a weapon, but *he'd be mighty tempted to make a fool of himself somehow.*

Georgia said she wanted an honest man. Well, he'd blown it up to this point, but he could at least be honest about how he felt about her.

Turning a smile toward the good doctor, he said, "As a matter of fact, Doc, there *is* something you can do for me."

GEORGIA LEANED on the exam table, trying to collect herself.

"Hey, are you okay?"

She looked up to see that Toni had poked her head into the room. Georgia sighed and nodded. "What are you doing down here?"

"I had a break and I thought maybe you could use one, too."

"Could I ever." Georgia averted her gaze from her friend's quizzical look as they headed toward the break room.

"Well, I thought you'd be glad to know that I just told Dr. Baxter that my name isn't Terri."

She managed a smile. "Good for you. What did he say?"

Toni grinned. "He said the only way he could remember the name Toni was to think of Italian food—you know, like rigatoni. Oh, and would I like to have dinner with him?"

Despite her own recent romantic disasters, Georgia was happy for her friend. "I knew you'd get your man."

Toni's smile dimmed. "Okay, Georgia, 'fess up. What's wrong?"

Georgia glanced around, then said, "Ken stopped by."

"No kidding? What did he say?"

She grunted. "Same thing—that he was sorry."

"Maybe he is."

"Well, that's not good enough."

"Georgia, what do you want him to say?"

She frowned. "Nothing. I want him to stay away from me."

"Are you sure?"

She fed coins into a soda machine. "After what he did?"

"I'm not taking up for the guy, but anyone can make a mistake."

"Toni, a mistake is adding two numbers wrong. The man has a fundamental character flaw—he's a self-centered jerk who doesn't care about other people." She blinked back a wall of sudden tears. "He certainly doesn't care about me."

A voice she recognized as Dr. Story's came over the intercom. "Please stand by for an important message."

She winced. She'd forgotten to stop by for her personal copy of her official reprimand. What a fun errand *that* would be.

"Georgia, this is Ken."

She missed her mouth and spilled her soda down the front of her scrubs.

Toni stared at her wide-eyed. "He's on the inter-
om."

"I love you," he said, his voice strong and resonat-
ng. "I don't expect this to change your mind, I just wanted you to know."

Georgia dropped the can and allowed Toni to scramble for it while she processed Ken's revelation. She heard muted applause in the halls, and several people walked by the vending room, giving her the thumbs-up.

"What are you going to do?" Toni screeched, jumping up and down.

She shook her head. "He doesn't mean it."

"Are you crazy? The man told you he loved you over the intercom, for heaven's sake!"

"He's just trying to ease his conscience. Men like Ken Medlock will say anything when they're backed into a corner." She should know—she'd seen her father's sugary words and elaborate gifts melt her mother's resolve. Well, she'd rather be alone the rest of her life than submit to a man on whom love would be wasted.

"You're simply going to ignore him?"

Georgia fed more coins into the vending machine, albeit with shakier fingers. "That's right. I'm simply going to ignore him."

At least she would try.

25

GEORGIA STARED at the report in her hand, her official reprimand for "treating a canine in a human health facility." Her own signature looked timid next to Dr. Story's flourishing script.

"Destroy them," Dr. Story had said, handing her both the original that had been bound for her file and a copy. "Officer Medlock came by Saturday morning to explain the situation, and I realize I acted in haste."

She pursed her mouth. Ken's timing surprised her—before their closet encounter, and before she found out about his little "impersonation." Walking to the kitchen trash can, she tore the papers into several pieces before pitching them. She really didn't want to dwell on it too much, though, else she might start thinking Ken Medlock was a good guy after all.

The phone rang, startling her. She was tempted to let it roll over, but decided she wasn't going to allow the possibility of the caller being Ken to influence her phone habits. The sooner her life got back to normal, the boring off she'd be. She frowned. The *better* off she'd be. *Better*.

Ignoring her Freudian slip, she picked up the handset. "Hello?"

She held her breath, and for a split second, God help her, she wanted it to be him.

"Hello, dear, it's Mother."

Shaking her head, she smiled at Arletta Adams's uncanny sense of timing. And absolutely no respect for the time difference from Denver to Birmingham. Not that it mattered, since Georgia couldn't sleep. "Hi, Mom." She dropped onto the couch, no doubt bruising her backside. She wondered vaguely where Ken had gotten his big comfy couches.

"I called to see if you and Bob had fun at the wedding."

She sighed. "Actually, Mom, Bob didn't make it."

"Oh, that's too bad. Why not?"

"It doesn't matter, really. We broke up."

"Oh, honey, I'm sorry. What happened?"

"I realized…that I didn't care for him as much as I thought." She reached for the envelope of photos she'd had developed, and pulled out one she'd taken at the park. Crash was the main focus, his head resting on the side of the wagon, but the lens had captured Ken in the top corner, leaning forward, his cheeks pushed up in a grand smile, his hair slightly ruffled in the wind. The darn viewfinder on the camera was obviously skewed.

"Well, as pretty as you are, you're bound to meet a wonderful man soon. Did you check out the groomsmen?"

She laughed. "No."

Her mother sighed, a musical little sound to the tune of "you missed another chance." "Weddings are a good place to meet eligible men, Georgia."

That smile. She loved that smile. Georgia rubbed her forefinger over his face. Such a nice face. "Now that you mention it, Mom, I did meet someone at the wedding."

By the silence, she knew she had her mother's attention. "Who?"

"His name is Ken," she said before she could stop the words. "Ken Medlock. It's funny, because he reminds me a little of Daddy." Georgia remained stock still, wondering what her mother's reaction would be.

"That's wonderful, dear."

"Is it, Mom? Is it really?"

Her mother sighed, an earnest one, this time, and Georgia sensed a change in her. "Georgia, your father wasn't perfect, but I loved him. Do I wish things had been different? Of course I do. I wish *I* had been different."

She didn't want to hear her mother accepting blame for her father's shenanigans. "Mom—"

"I hated sex, Georgia."

She swallowed her words, and her eyes bugged. "Oh."

"It was inevitable that your father stray. The few times he did, I didn't like it, but I didn't blame him. And he never stopped loving me."

She clasped a hand to her forehead, stunned at her mother's revelation. "All these years, I thought that he was hurting you."

"Quite the opposite, dear. Your father and I loved each other deeply. He always felt so guilty about his affairs that he brought me gifts. I never doubted his commitment to our family."

In thirty seconds, her entire outlook on sex and relationships had been turned on end. "I don't know what to say."

"Then tell me about this Ken Medlock, dear."

Georgia's mind raced with images of Ken, so many of them jammed into only a few days, and all of them...profound.

"Georgia, what does the man do?"

She pressed the picture of Ken to her heart, and closed her eyes. "He makes me happy, Mom. Can I call you back?"

"Of course, dear."

She hung up and brought her fist to her mouth. Her father had indulged in extra-marital affairs because her mother hated sex. Not because one woman wasn't enough for him. Not because he enjoyed seeing how much he could get away with. Not because he didn't love his family. Her mother had violated her marriage vows first, by not honoring the physical needs of her husband. Georgia had sorely misjudged her father. She sent up a prayer of apology and a smile to the man she'd always adored, but whose situation she had never fully appreciated.

A warm, fuzzy feeling flooded over her, along with a revelation: Perhaps her father had orchestrated the chance meeting with Ken. The sequence of events seemed almost too fantastic for mere mortal coincidence. She smiled. He was still looking out for her. Fannie had Mother, and she had Dad.

So she hadn't inherited dark, lusty, philandering tendencies. Her sex drive had been kicked into overdrive by a man whom she'd been destined to meet. A man who stirred her soul before she even knew him.

A man to whom she was drawn both physically and metaphysically.

Georgia counted to ten to calm her pounding heart. She loved Ken. It was impossible, but true. They'd connected so quickly and so intensely that she'd been frightened. Since it seemed too good to be true, she'd been poised for the other shoe to drop. And it had, when she'd found out it was him she'd been talking to on the phone, him she'd been sharing her thoughts and fantasies with. But on some subconscious level, hadn't she wished it were Ken all along?

She was being handed a gift on one of those platters she wanted. She would not turn from love and run.

She looked at the phone and laughed aloud when she realized his number was still programmed in. She pushed the button, then his phone rang once, twice as her heart nearly jumped out of her chest. Was he home? It was awfully late. Was he asleep? Would he be glad to hear from her?

"Hello," he said, and his voice filled her chest with warmth.

"Ken, it's Georgia."

"Hi," he said, sounding glad, but tentative. "It's great to hear your voice. I didn't think—"

"I love you, too."

Strangling sounds came across the line.

"Are you choking?" she asked. "Because I know the Heimlich maneuver."

He laughed. "So you say."

"I was wondering if you know where I live."

"Yes, ma'am, I do."

She smiled wryly. Of course he did. "Well, in that

case, I was wondering if you would like to come over."

She heard a loud popping noise, as if the phone had been dropped. "Ken?"

From the rhythmic knocking sound, she realized the handset was dangling and swinging back and forth against something. She laughed into the phone as she heard his door slam.

Georgia hugged herself, hoping that Ken had the cruiser and would turn on the blue lights. She hated to wait.

Epilogue

"THE NEXT TIME we get married," Ken whispered against the back of her neck, "Pick a wedding gown that has fewer buttons."

"All the better to torture you, my dear," she murmured with a smile, rolling her shoulders in response to the delicious thrill of his tongue. "Ken, I was thinking."

"Hmm?"

She turned in his arms and tugged at the lapels of his black tuxedo jacket. "Since we have the rest of our lives to make love while I'm *not* wearing my wedding gown, why don't we—"

He grabbed her around the waist, grinning. "I like the way you think, Mrs. Medlock."

He carried her to the bed in the luxurious honeymoon suite they'd reserved and set her on the edge. She started to slip off her shoes, but he stopped her, pushing her gently back on the bed. He then removed the satin heels with much ado, and kissed his way up to the top of her white thigh-high stockings.

Just knowing the pleasures that lay ahead had her writhing against the covers. "Blue lights, Ken," she whispered, their private shorthand when one of them could barely wait for the other to love them.

His laugh was throaty as he unfastened his waistband. "I love it when you talk dirty, ma'am."

"Oh, but isn't this better than phone sex?" She moaned as he entered her, swift and hard.

"Is it ever," he breathed against her neck. "I love you, Georgia."

"I love you, too," she panted, meeting his long, filling strokes. Her climax was close, and he knew it.

His face glistened with perspiration as he talked to her, murmuring sizzling, erotic words. Her thighs burned with the need for her release. He drew her knees up and levered himself over her, driving deep, bringing her to the brink, then over, in a rhythmic flood of ecstasy. She cried out his name over and over. His orgasm intensified hers as he expanded and pulsed inside her.

Georgia moaned and smiled to herself as he eased his head down to her shoulder. At this rate, they'd be pregnant by tomorrow. "Ken?"

"Hmm?"

She laughed, fanning herself. "The next time we get married, can it not be in the middle of a heat wave?"

He lifted himself on his elbows, his eyes sensuously glazed. "But since we met in a heat wave, I thought it was only appropriate. Besides," he said, nipping at her neck in preparation for round two, "a heat wave is the best time for lovers."

"Why?"

Ken growled against her neck. "Because it's too hot to sleep."

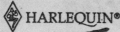